I0687512

Juelle's Legacy

by

Carol Henry

The Lobster Cove Series

Juelle's Legacy

Cover Art by *Tina Lynn Stout*

The Wild Rose Press, Inc.
PO Box 708
Adams Basin, NY 14410-0708
Visit us at www.thewildrosepress.com

Publishing History
First Champagne Rose Edition, 2014
Print ISBN 978-1-62830-571-5
Digital ISBN 978-1-62830-572-2

The Lobster Cove Series
Published in the United States of America

Juelle had all she could do to hold back her own tears. Could she do it? Could she tell the doctors to let her husband go? And if she did, would it be murder, as Eugenia accused? She lowered her head and shut her eyes before her tears could fall. She fisted her hands, and took several deep breaths, swallowed. God, she was tired of holding it all in.

She swung away from the scene in front of her, and headed for the door, only to be brought up short by a man standing there as if he'd been gob-struck. The man she'd seen at Mariner's the night before blocked her exit. Before she could ask why he was here, Eugenia's gasp drew her attention back to her mother-in-law. Clasping the back of a chair, the woman looked ready to pass out. Eugenia recovered so fast, Juelle wondered if she had imagined her mother-in-law's reaction.

"What the hell are you doing here? Get him out of here. *He! Is! Not! Family!*" Eugenia screeched.

Juelle did a double-take. If she considered Eugenia sounded like a banshee before, with her ear splitting shrieking, her tone now was so venomous it had everyone stopping in their tracks and staring in disbelief. The strange man was the first to recover. He walked into the enclosed room. Juelle recognized the astonishment in his pinched lips, raised eyebrows.

"I *am* family." His voice was calm, well-modulated, and confident. "Allow me to introduce myself—Hunter McClintock. I assume you know my father?"

Juelle's mouth dropped. She couldn't form a single sane word. Eugenia, however, had no trouble.

"Liar! Hunt McClintock's *only* son is lying in that bed."

Praise for Carol Henry's Books

NOTHING SHORT OF A MIRACLE

"Carol Henry is a gifted writer who paints you a picture of all the fine details of the season. A master at pacing...the ins and outs of the developing romance are a delight to read...The story is like a warm hug."

~*W. A. Darling, 25 Days of Christmas Stories Review*

~*~

AMAZON CONNECTION

"...a fast paced suspense that will have you reading as fast as possible to get to the next page. The description of the Amazon jungle will make you feel like you are actually there."

~*You Gotta Read Reviews*

~*~

SHANGHAI CONNECTION

Voted #2 Best Book/E-Book Romance Novel 2012
Preditors & Editors Reader's Poll

~*~

"Carol Henry's beautifully written descriptions immerse you in the surroundings where there are plenty of edge-of-the-seat thrills...a connection you want to make!"

~*Mal Olson, author of adrenaline-kicked romantic suspense*

~*~

"Rich with setting and suspense...Carol Henry brings the setting alive with lush, vivid descriptions...and keeps you turning pages until the very end."

~*Alicia Dean, romantic suspense author*

Dedication

To my high school sweetheart,
my hero,
and my very best friend and travel buddy
—my husband Gary.

Chapter One

Hunter McClintock sat back in the wicker chair on the veranda and stared at the return address on the envelope he held in his hand. Lobster Cove, Maine. The tropical Oahu breeze did little to cool the afternoon heat—and his insides. After all these years, his estranged father's lawyer, Günter Jordan, was contacting him. It could only mean one thing—his father had died.

"Before you open the envelope, son, we need to talk." Lani Aka McClintock stepped out onto the patio of her home overlooking the wide expanse of the Pacific Ocean. She carried a tray of iced tea, which she placed on the glass top covering the small, round table. "Fresh tea, with lemons from the plantation down the road." She poured from an iced pitcher dripping in moisture from the heat, and handed him a tall frothy tumbler before serving herself. She rounded the table, brushed her long, straight black hair behind her ears, and then sat down opposite him. The red and white frilled umbrella overhead shaded them from the bright afternoon sun.

"It's okay, Mom. I know it's about my father. I'm no longer a hostile youth, angry that I didn't have a father to teach me sports, or follow my games. I had you." He couldn't have asked for a more supportive and loving parent. And he'd had his mother's family—all his aunts, uncles, and cousins.

He grinned, leaned across the table, and patted his mother's hand. He was pleased to see her smile. His mother was a beautiful Hawaiian, tiny, petite, but a dynamo when it came to running their travel agency. She was well respected in her business, and by her family.

Hunter looked at the envelope and shook his head. "Why would anyone from my father's family want to contact me now?"

"Your father is a wealthy man. He owns a fishing company he inherited from his father—Herman McClintock. I understand he was a hard man to cross. McClintock and McClintock was a large concern back when we married. I'm sure he's made the lobster business a world class industry by now. Hunt travelled to Hawaii for his father—looking for connections to expand the business."

"Is that how you met? You never did tell me."

"You were too young to understand, and then you were too old to care."

"Well, I'm old enough to know and care now."

"Hunt was wandering the beach the day we met." Her nostalgic smile zinged his insides. He shouldn't have encouraged her to tell him.

"I was collecting shells along the shore. We fell in love so fast—had a love affair, and were married within the week. A week later, his father demanded Hunt return to Maine. He left, said he'd return for me. But I never saw him again."

Hunter saw the sadness in her eyes, and once again, wanted to do bodily harm to his father, were he alive.

"I wrote to Hunt—told him I was pregnant. I

received a letter from Herman saying he'd had our marriage annulled. That Hunt had remarried and his wife was with child. Apparently, our letters crossed in the mail. I never heard from the McClintocks again."

Hunter laid the envelope on the table, took a long swallow of iced tea, welcoming the coolness as it trickled down his parched throat. He looked out at the shimmering ocean and the frothy waves slapping against the white sand along the beach. A few gulls swooped down looking for a meal. The calmness of it all did nothing for his jittery stomach. He didn't want his mother to see how unnerving this letter really was— what it represented to him. A connection. A connection he had longed to receive over the past twenty-eight years. And now it was too late—he'd never have the opportunity to speak to his father—or his grandfather.

"I don't need to open it. It means nothing to me now. At one time, I yearned for a letter from him, but no longer. I have all I need right here in Oahu."

"Open it. You will always wonder what it said if you don't. Face your fears, son, and go forward. But keep an open perspective."

Fears? He'd faced worse things than worrying about opening a damn envelope—he'd served his country in Afghanistan. It had put his life in perspective. Not having a father around didn't even come close to the suffering he'd seen over there. He'd fought with the best of them, protected those around him, and they'd saved his ass more than a few times. Why, then did he dread opening this envelope?

He rubbed an unsteady hand over his face and took a deep breath. He had the strangest notion the contents were about to change his life. Upset the proverbial apple cart. He glanced at his mother. She bit down on her lower lip, a sure indication she was as nervous as he was about the letter's contents. Her worried frown pierced his heart. She hadn't been well the past month—the flu had set her back for days. He cursed his estranged father for the umpteenth millionth time. *Dammit!* If he didn't open the letter, she would be more worried about not knowing its contents than he would. This letter from Lobster Cove was about to tear her heart apart—he could only hope it would be for the last time.

Hunter cursed his father, leaned forward, and lifted the envelope from the table. He slit the top edge open, withdrew a single sheet of tan, embossed bond stationary, unfolded it, and read the contents in silence.

"It's from Jordan and Jordan, Attorneys at Law, Lobster Cove, Maine." He lowered the letter to his lap. "Hunter McClintock, Senior died almost a year ago. I'm sorry, Mom."

Tears trickled down her cheeks. *Oh, crap.* He hadn't expected tears. Was she still in love with the man after all these years? If Hunt McClintock was standing here, right now, he'd kill the S.O.B. with his bare hands.

He rushed to her side and put his arms around her thin shoulders—her tiny frame barely filled the chair.

"You still loved him, didn't you, Mom? After all these years you never let go? Is that why you've never remarried?"

"Yes. I loved him. How could I not? He gave me you." She stood, crossed the deck to the railing and looked out over the glittering expanse of water. "For that, I have always been grateful. I had you to raise, and love. After he left—you were...are...my life, son. I have no regrets."

She brushed the back of her hand over her tear-filled eyes and straightened her shoulders. He joined her and together they continued to look out over the tropical seascape—a hedgerow of deep pink bougainvillea grew in profusion before sloping down to the beachfront where several palm trees stood to the right, their fronds bending in the breeze. Light foaming waves washed up on the shore.

"They want you to go to Lobster Cove, am I right?"

"Yes, but it's too late. If Hunter McClintock, Senior is dead, there is no need for me to travel that far for something I don't want."

"Yes. There is. You must go. You must lay your bitterness to rest. Find out what they want." She patted his hand as if to pacify him when she was the one who needed consoling. It had been years since he'd given his father a second thought. Why the hell were they opening up old wounds now? Making him think about things best left alone?

"What good does it do, now? There is nothing I want from him. Nothing."

"You won't know unless you go and find out."

"Not without you. They want you there, as well."

"I'm not up to a long plane ride right now. This flu business has made me too weak. Besides, I am sure there is absolutely nothing there I want, nor would I be welcome."

"And you think I will be welcomed?" Hunter snorted a laugh. What a joke. He was the last person Hunt McClintock's family would want to show up on their doorstep.

"When are you expected?"

"We…when are we expected. Next week."

"I am not in a position to travel so far right now. Nor do I have the heart to go. The travel agency will be fine while you are gone. Uncle Eddie is scheduled to handle the tours to the Big Island next week. Aunt Lydia has the extra tours booked through the month. I will ask her to make a few changes, rearrange our guides on a few of the longer tours. You can do double tours when you return."

He was loath to reply. But if it would ease his mother's mind, he would go. Get it over with once and for all. He only wished she was well enough to take the trip to the mainland with him.

Chapter Two

Juelle McClintock sat next to her husband's hospital bed in the dimly lit I.C.U. room, held his limp hand, and prayed he would recover. She cursed the fishing accident that left him in this coma. She cursed him for taking the trawler out during one of the worst storms Lobster Cove had seen in over a century. His usual rugged good looks were absent. Lifeless, eyes closed, his once wavy, flighty hair lay limp. Beneath his fisherman's tan was a pale reflection of the adventuresome man she had fallen in love with in college—he'd swept her off her feet with his alluring charms. Was it only two years ago?

Hooked up to numerous tubes and equipment, as well as a central venous catheter, and an I.V. in his arm, making it hard for Juelle to get close enough without disturbing all the connections. She managed to lean in next to him. She brushed strands of hair away from his ear as if it would make hearing her that much better.

"Sebastian, if you can hear me, please, try to squeeze my hand. Move something. Anything. Give me a sign you can hear me. Something to let me know you're going to be okay. I'm here. You're not alone. *Please*." Juelle spoke slow and clear, hoping he heard. The tube down his throat prevented him from speaking, but she remained as close as possible in case he attempted to do something—anything. She didn't want to miss a single sound, or movement.

She waited.

Nothing.

The doctors hadn't held out much hope he would come out of the coma, but she couldn't give up on him. Even though their relationship had started to disintegrate soon after they had moved in with his parents at the McClintock Estate. Thinking their marriage would improve once Makenzie was born had been wishful thinking on her part. She'd been the only one to try to make it work. But she had to stay by Sebastian's side—he was still her husband. She promised to work harder at their marriage—make things better when he snapped out of this coma. She would learn to be more understanding and not force the issue of finding a place of their own, to understand his mother's personality, her point of view.

She rubbed his hand—the one without anything attached. Discouraged, she leaned back in the chair, then bent forward, and rested her forehead on the edge of the bed. The sheet, cool and soothing against her balmy skin, did little to take away the turmoil churning inside. She sighed. Her eyes drifted shut. Would he ever come out of this coma? Recover? She took another deep breath, let it out. A few more minutes and she'd leave to go pick up Makenzie from her best friend's house.

"You'd better be praying. It's the least you can do."

Juelle's head shot up.

"Eugenia! Sorry, I didn't hear you come in. Is it five-thirty already?" Juelle stood to face her mother-in-law, her head dizzy from jumping up so fast. She brushed the hair off her forehead with shaky fingers, straightened her cotton tank-top over her black slacks, and bushed her hands down the side of her thighs. Why she let her mother-in-law make her so nervous, she didn't know, or understand. She wasn't a wuss, could stand up for herself and Makenzie. But Eugenia McClintock was one of those women who wouldn't be denied.

"Has my son shown any signs of movement yet? Opened his eyes while I wasn't here? Called out for me? Don't be keeping it from me if he did. I'm his mother—I have a right to know."

"Of course you do. I would never keep something as important as that from you."

"Let me see for myself."

Eugenia trudged to the bedside, effectively blocking Juelle's access to Sebastian's side. She stepped back to keep her foot from being crushed underneath her mother-in-law's sharp heels. The woman was a fashion plate, right down to her shoes—it didn't matter if she was only going to the grocery store or a meeting. She was pulled together from head to toe.

"Sebastian!" her mother-in-law bellowed in her son's face. "Sebastian! Wake up!"

"Yelling isn't going to do any good. The doctors are adamant there isn't much hope he will recover. We have to accept their diagnosis." Juelle felt sorry for the young boy Sebastian had been, to have been raised by this domineering mother. Her own parents might not have been around much, but they weren't overbearing.

"Bah. What do the doctors know? People wake up from comas all the time. Besides, I do not want to lose my son—he's all I have left in the world."

"I know this is hard on you, especially after Hunt's death. But Sebastian is my husband, and seeing him laying here like this isn't any easier for me."

Her words had little impact on Eugenia's emotional state at the moment. She wasn't about to remind her mother-in-law that she had a granddaughter—Makenzie. The distraught woman still grieved over losing her own husband. Hunt McClintock's sudden heart attack at age fifty-nine had shocked the entire community of Lobster Cove. McClintock and McClintock Lobster Company employed the majority of the fishermen in town. He was well liked and treated his employees well. With his son near death, the status of the company was uncertain. If Sebastian should die, who would assume control?

"You have no idea what I am going through," Eugenia huffed, her hands on her hips, her head thrown back, and her hazel eyes as glacial as winter ice on the edges of Frenchman Bay.

Juelle took a deep breath.

"Eugenia. I don't want to argue with you in front of Sebastian—whether he can hear us or not. I'm sure if he does snap out of his coma he wouldn't want it to be because of our raised voices." She inched her way to the door. "I have to pick up Makenzie—Katelyn has to be at Mariner's by six for the evening shift. I'll leave you to be with your son."

"Don't forget we have a historical society meeting at seven tonight."

How could she forget? Eugenia had it marked on all three calendars, posted sticky notes next to the phone in the hall and on the refrigerator. The woman was an organizational wizard and kept all her community functions straight. But with everything Juelle had been through, she planned on skipping tonight's meeting, which was sure to put another nail in her coffin if Eugenia had anything to do with it.

The late afternoon sun shifted over the western border of Mount Desert Island, leaving Lobster Cove in shadow. The cool breeze off Frenchman Bay tossed Juelle's shoulder-length hair about as she pulled her lime-green VW Beetle into the drive in front of Katelyn's cottage. Sebastian had wanted her to buy a sportier car, something more showy and in line with their status in the community, but she refused. She wanted a small, dependable vehicle—something down to earth. She got out, pocketed her keys, and made her way up the sidewalk to pick up Makenzie. Katelyn's small cottage was tucked into a stand of Aspen and Birch on the edge of town, closer to Bar Harbor. The side street jutted off Main Street, and although there were other cottages nearby, Katelyn's had the advantage of being the last one on the block. An assorted color of lupines lined the front of the house. She would give anything to live in one of these cottages, no matter how small. Just to be able to leave her mother-in-law's home would be a godsend.

Before Juelle could knock, her best friend, Katelyn, opened the screen door. A tall blonde, with sexy hazel eyes and a model's body, her friend greeted her with Makenzie in her arms. Makenzie clapped her hands and held them out for Juelle, a wide toothless smile on her chubby cheeks. Juelle took her daughter in her arms. Her baby snuggled, tucked her head in Juelle's neck, and hummed. Her heart melted. She kissed her daughter on the forehead, hugged her again, and then followed

Katelyn inside.

"You didn't have to rush to pick up this precious girl. We were having such a great time—weren't we, sweetie? We were just about to finish our tea party. You can join us."

Makenzie gurgled and clapped her hands, again.

"Are you sure? Don't you have to be at your parent's diner at six? I don't want to hold you up." Katelyn's parents, Roark and Dawn Sullivan, had owned Mariner's Fish Fry, located on the northern end of the harbor, for over twenty years.

"The good thing about working for my parents is, a start time is when I get there. They aren't going anywhere in a hurry tonight—they don't want to miss out on the evening crowd—all their regulars will be rolling in for tonight's lobster roll special."

Katelyn led them into a small room off the sitting room. A small children's table was set for tea with a pink Disney tea set—all the princesses depicted on each diminutive tea cup, saucer, tea pot, and sugar and creamer—every little girl's dream.

"Have a seat. I'm afraid your knees might hit your chin, but Makenzie fits just right in these chairs, don't you, darling?"

Makenzie smiled and clapped her hands.

"This is so adorable. Where did you find this?"

"It was mine when I was a little girl."

"Aren't you afraid Makenzie will break something?"

"If you look close enough, you'll see the cup handles have already been glued back on a couple of times. Not to worry, I have plenty of glue in the cupboard if I need it."

Juelle settled her daughter in the chair beside her, while Katelyn poured tea for the three of them. Three small peanut butter cookies were displayed in another princess dish in the center of the table. Makenzie helped herself. Juelle smiled. Katelyn passed the cream and sugar.

"I can't thank you enough for babysitting Makenzie and not plunking her in front of a television. It's encouraging to have someone spend time with her while I can't."

"You know I love having her. She's a darling baby, and so well behaved. You've done a wonderful job raising her."

"She's a joy. Despite what's going on between Sebastian and me, Makenzie is a comfort—she keeps me going—literally."

The two of them laughed and Makenzie joined in, as if she understood what they were talking about.

"So, how was Sebastian today? Any change?" Katelyn lifted her tiny cup and sipped.

"No," Juelle sighed. "I'm worried, though. The doctors aren't holding out much hope."

"What about Eugenia? How is she doing?"

"Eugenia doesn't change. She's just as difficult as ever. I know it's her son, and she's still grieving for her husband, which she has no problem reminding me at every turn. But I am so tired of trying to appease her every time I turn around. And I'm not ecstatic over the possibility of losing my husband regardless of our problems."

"According to my mother, Eugenia's had a hard life. Coming from a poor immigrant family, she was raised by foster families and didn't have much of an advantage growing up. Her father worked as a fisherman for the McClintock's—it's how she met Hunt. Guess she didn't know how to handle falling head over heels into wealth."

"An understatement. The woman never lets anyone forget she has money. It's obvious the way she throws it around and makes a big deal over it. At least it all goes to worthy causes—I've got to give her that."

They both paused to sip tea, fawn over Makenzie, who was having a hard time keeping tea from spilling down the front of her lavender sundress. Thankful Katelyn had covered her daughter with a full-length cloth bib—her dress was safe from stains. Makenzie kicked her legs and giggled, then plunked the cup back on the table. Juelle cringed, lifted it up for inspection, hoping it hadn't cracked.

"She's fine." Katelyn smiled and waved her hand. "Relax. You're wound too tight. Why don't you join us at Mariner's tonight? Bring Makenzie along and have dinner with the family. They'd be glad to see you."

"I can't. Eugenia reminded me we have a historical society meeting at seven. Heaven forbid if I'm late. Although I am tempted to stay home tonight."

"You can miss one meeting."

Juelle considered the consequences. "I'd better not. Eugenia is going through a lot right now. I don't want to give her anything more to get upset over. Maybe another time."

"The meeting isn't until seven—you can at least come have a lobster roll before you go. It'll do you good to get out and about besides spending all your time at the hospital. I won't take no for an answer. Let's clean up this little lady and get ready. I'll clear up this tea mess later."

****

Hunter pulled his black Kia rental into Frenchman Bay Motel's parking lot lined with trimmed boxwood. The motel was a long, two-story white establishment with Kelly-green shutters, situated on a knoll overlooking the harbor. A wide porch circled the building with doors and windows for easy access to the individual rooms from the outside. A single Adirondack chair sat on either side of each door. According to the Web, the motel had been in the family for two generations, and once housed the rich and famous. The French family had turned it into a motel to accommodate the overflow of visitors to the island, Acadia National Park, and Bar Harbor. He turned off his GPS, retrieved his single luggage from the back seat, and then climbed the four carpeted steps to the entrance. Once inside, the homey, cozy ambiance of the motel was a welcome sight. Not as open as the hotels and smaller touristy establishments in Oahu, but friendly and comfortable looking.

"May I help you?" a teenage girl, about five feet even, with a long ponytail sitting behind the desk inquired. A table to the right offered coffee, an iced drink of some sort, and a platter of cookies. Just to the side was an assortment of travel brochures.

"Yes, please. McClintock. Hunter McClintock. I have a reservation."

"Oh my! McClintock? Are you related to the McClintocks who own the lobster company here in Lobster Cove?"

He wasn't sure how to answer. He didn't want to cause a stir in this small community, and he wasn't going to be here long. He hesitated, dug through his wallet for his credit card, and handed it over the counter, dodging the question.

"I'm just in from Oahu, thinking about checking out the island. I hear Acadia National Park is well worth the visit."

"Well, now, you've traveled a long way just to visit the park. But you'll love it. All the visitors do. And there is so much to see and do here in Lobster Cove. Not sure how long you're going to be here, but next weekend is Father's Day. The Oil and Water Art Festival showcases Maine's art and artists. It takes place in the park next to the harbor."

How ironic that he should arrive in Lobster Cove in time for an event highlighting Father's Day—a day he'd ignored most of his life. When he was younger, he'd envied the other kids talking about their fathers and the special things they did together. Later, it had become just another day of the year. He'd spend his Sunday surfing with his friends, or hiking alone along Waimea Canyon. And now, to be here over Father's Day for the reading of his father's will, a father he never knew, well shit, it brought a lump to his throat all over again. The timing couldn't be worse.

"Of course many people start out visiting Bar Harbor," the receptionist was saying.

He smiled and hoped she hadn't noticed his rudeness. Apparently not—she continued.

"But to come all this way and leave Hawaii behind? Hawaii is *the* most romantic place on earth. I'm hoping to visit there someday."

The young girl almost swooned when she said it. Hunter smiled and shook his head. The Hawaiian

Islands did have a reputation for having a romantic effect on the majority of the people from the mainland. He'd seen it a million times as he'd guided tours on the various islands back home. He didn't blame them. No matter which island he visited, it was sheer paradise. He couldn't imagine living anywhere else. Including Lobster Cove, Maine.

"You'll have to visit someday. I'm sure you'll enjoy it."

"I sure hope so. Here you go, Mr. McClintock." She handed him a small packet across the counter. "Room eight, down at the end. You'll have more privacy there and be closer to the harbor sights. Breakfast is early here—six until nine-thirty. I'm Gigi. My parents Jolie and Russ French own the motel. Let one of us know if you need anything. If no one is at the desk, just ring the bell." She pointed to an old-fashioned, servant-type silver bell.

"Can you recommend a good place to have a bite to eat tonight?"

"The best place around for a fresh lobster dinner and homemade blueberry pie is at Mariner's Fish Fry just down the road and around the corner on the opposite side of the bay. Can't miss it. It's on the harbor. Roark and Dawn Sullivan own it. Best lobster rolls and blueberry muffins in town, too."

"Thanks. Appreciate your help."

Hunter pocketed the key card, grabbed his luggage, and then headed down the veranda to his room. He inserted the card into the door lock and entered the darkened room. He placed his travel bag on the small easy chair next to the table and sat on the edge of the bed. The mattress was firm, the bedspread crisp, and the scent of fresh balsam filled the room. He took out his cell phone and called his mother to let her know he'd arrived in Lobster Cove. He looked around the room while he waited for her to pick up. At the far end was an alcove with a dressing table and sink, to the left was a door, which led into a bathroom complete with a walk-in shower.

His mother's phone clicked to the answering machine—he left a brief message to let her know he'd arrived without a hitch. He'd contact her later, after he'd met with the lawyer. He then dialed the number for Jordan and Jordan, Attorneys at Law, to set up an appointment. The sooner he got this over with, the better.

****

Juelle pulled into the side of Mariner's Fish Fry parking lot and parked the car in the one remaining spot out front. The Sullivan family had owned the establishment from the beginning of time and was a popular place. Many of the fishermen who worked at McClintock's frequented the place. It was more than a local dive—it was a well-established restaurant despite the name of the business.

Juelle lifted the entire car seat, with Makenzie in it, out of the car, flicked the handle into position turning it into a carry seat, and made her way to the restaurant. To the left of the blue and white building was a short, squatty lighthouse with a deck circling the second floor. The light in the top still functioned, although it was more for show than to warn ships approaching shore. The real lighthouse was on the other side of the harbor. The main diner's elongated portion stretched out toward the road, sported a peaked roof, and displayed an assortment of colorful hanging licensed lobster buoys along the roof's edge for decoration. Old wooden lobster traps and nets were stacked against the building, giving it a definite working harbor flavor. The entrance's green canopy was emblazoned with a large red lobster and the name of the diner in white underneath.

Katelyn met her at the front steps, and the three entered the diner together. Katelyn's mother greeted them as she rushed past, carrying a large platter with a fresh steamed lobster, corn on the cob, and an impressive portion of coleslaw on the side.

"Hi, Juelle. I see you have your darling girl with you today. Give me a minute, and I'll be right with you. Go find a seat while I deliver this dinner."

"Thanks, Mrs. Sullivan. I'll go sit out back on the deck."

"I'm heading there now. Pick up a menu on your way out."

"I'm going to have dinner with Juelle, if you don't mind, Mom. Then I'm all yours for the rest of the night."

Mrs. Sullivan, nodded, paused, and made her way out to the deck overlooking the bay. The scent of fresh seafood filled the room as they followed Katelyn's mother out back. Juelle's stomach growled, the little sip of tea with Makenzie and Katelyn a short while ago hadn't satisfied her hunger. She'd spent most of the day at the hospital. Lunch had been a long time gone, and coffee was no substitute, the caffeine only aggravating the hunger pangs churning around in her stomach.

Once settled at one of the many picnic tables lining the back deck, Juelle set the carry seat on the table top, and took a moment to look out over the harbor and the bay beyond. She never grew tired of the seaside harbor view with the lobster and fishing boats tied up at the piers, the private yachts and sailboats coming and going. This time of night, with a few lights sparkling off the water, and the lights from around the deck glittering, a warm, romantic feeling tugged her heartstrings. She sighed, wishing she and Sebastian would be able to regain that special feeling they shared when they'd first met.

"What are you up for tonight?" Katelyn opened the menu and started reading down the list. "Scallops are great, if I do say so myself. Claude said the men managed to catch some good looking specimens late this afternoon."

"I think I'll go with just a lobster roll. Easier to eat while I feed Makenzie."

"They are delicious—sweet and filling. Sit and relax. I'll go put in our order."

After Katelyn went inside, Juelle sighed, and then scanned the back deck as the evening crowd gathered. The man to the left, three tables down where Mrs. Sullivan had delivered the lobster meal, looked familiar. She couldn't place him and was still trying to figure it out when her friend returned.

"Good-looking, isn't he? Mom said he was new in town. He's staying at the Frenchman Bay Motel. Here, I got us a soda and a juice cup for Makenzie while we wait for our meal." She joined Juelle on the opposite side of the table and looked down past the row of tables already filling up for the night.

"He does look familiar, but I can't place him."

"Love the tan and the dark hair. Looks like he

20

works out. Wonder where he's from? Mom says the place is buzzing trying to figure it out."

"Really, Katelyn? You're engaged to Sven, remember? I'm sure this guy is just a tourist."

"Almost engaged. Doesn't mean I can't look. Anyway, I want to know when you plan to vacate that rattle-trap of an estate and get a place of your own. It must be hard living alone with Eugenia while Sebastian is in the hospital. I don't mean to be insensitive, Juelle, but it's been two years."

"I was positive I had Sebastian talked into moving out, but then Makenzie was born, and then his father died, and poor Eugenia is having a hard time dealing with everything. I couldn't pack up and leave while she's under such stress. And now..., well..., if Sebastian doesn't make it..." Juelle bit her bottom lip, took a deep breath, and continued. "How can I take Makenzie away from her?"

"For your own sanity? I suggest you start making plans. The sooner the better. At least start looking."

"She's hurting. She needs more time to adjust. Besides, I haven't found an affordable place yet."

"Are you kidding me? With the income from McClintock and McClintock, Sebastian must be earning big bucks from the family business."

"I don't know. I've never seen his pay checks, only what he puts in our joint account at the bank."

"Here you go, ladies. Sorry it took so long, a bit backed up." Mrs. Sullivan gave her daughter the raised eyebrow.

"Sorry, Mom. I'll eat fast and be right there to pitch in. Juelle has a historical society meeting tonight, so we won't be long."

"Don't be a stranger, Juelle. You bring your darling girl in anytime. Waiting for Katelyn to give me grandkids is beginning to be a hopeless dream."

"Mom! I'm not even married yet."

"So what are you and that beau of yours waiting for?"

"Yeah, Katelyn. What are you two waiting for?"

"Not you too? Eat. You have a meeting to get to, remember?"

Chapter Three

Hunter entered the offices of Jordan and Jordan, Attorney at Law, on the corner of Birch and First Street. The receptionist, whose nameplate identified her as a Mrs. Carrie Saunders, greeted him and then pressed the intercom to announce his arrival. Mr. Jordan stepped out of his office down the hall.

"Mr. McClintock. Glad to finally meet you. Come in. Come in. Have a seat."

Günter Jordan was a tall, stocky man with a graying, receding hairline. His smile was genuine as he shook Hunter's hand in greeting—a firm, confident handshake. He motioned for Hunter to sit in the brown leather chair situated on the opposite side of his desk.

"I was surprised when I received your letter. In fact, it was rather a shock. I'm not sure why I'm here, but can only conclude my father—my estranged father—has died."

Günter Jordan shut the door and took his seat next to his small, but ornate desk. The bright Maine sunshine shone through the window directly behind the lawyer. Hunter was positive the man positioned his desk in such a manner in order to be intimidating, his facial expressions shadowed and hard to read. But Hunter wasn't about to be intimidated.

"I'm afraid you are correct in your assumption. We've had a hard time locating you and your mother, and now that we have, we can proceed with the reading of the will and put the family at ease."

"I can't believe it was so difficult to locate us. After all, my father knew exactly where my mother lived."

"Unfortunately, the information on your location wasn't available to us. Is your mother with you?"

"No. She isn't able to travel at the moment."

"I'm sorry to hear she couldn't make the trip. I hope it isn't anything serious."

"No. She'll be fine—a bit of flu, not to mention the shock of receiving your letter. Just needs to take it easy for a few weeks."

"Again. I'm sorry." The lawyer's sympathy appeared genuine. He settled in his office chair, cleared his throat, and looked down at the papers on his desk. "Now, about your father—"

"He never contacted me when he was alive, I don't see what my being here now is going to prove, other than stir things up with his current family. I assume he does have a family, am I right?"

"He does. However, be that as it may, I'm glad you are here. Hopefully, we will be able to get on with the reading of the will so his wife—his current wife— Eugenia McClintock—can deal with her current situation. Her son, Sebastian, who is your half-brother, was in a serious fishing accident several weeks ago, and is in a coma in the hospital. Although she has been anxious to deal with family issues, I have not been at liberty to divulge the contents of her husband's will. I can understand her concern. However, as the status of McClintock and McClintock Lobster Company is in question since Hunt McClintock's death and his son's accident, we need to get past this as soon as possible."

"Again, now that you know I refuse to accept anything my father may have designated for me, I fail to see why I should remain any longer. I have people counting on me back in Oahu." The room closed in on him—he stood up to leave. He was serious—he wanted nothing from a father who had no time for him while the man was alive.

"I understand you and your mother are owners of Lani Aloha Travel Agency. That she has never remarried."

Hunter sat back down. "I see you've done your homework. Impressive."

"That is what we do. Now, for the record, your father married Eugenia Craft and they had a child— Sebastian. Your half-brother. You have no other siblings."

Hunter wasn't surprised. His mother had warned him his father had remarried. Still, it hurt to think this half-brother had the advantage of growing up with a father—his father. How many Father's Days had they shared? Enjoyed?

Could his messed up family problems get any more complicated? Did he want to care that a half-brother he'd never met was in a coma?

"What is Sebastian's prognosis?" He didn't want to think that a part of him, family, was lying in the hospital near death. But curiosity surfaced, and as much as he was loath to accept he had a brother—a half-brother—he couldn't help but want to rush to his side. Were there other relatives nearby? Grandparents?

"I haven't had the official word, but it's my understanding his condition is not good. You might want to check with either his wife or mother."

No way was he about to search out Hunt's widow. In deference to his mother, he just couldn't do it. But a wife? The poor woman must be beside herself, grieving over her husband's sad state of affairs.

"Do you think that's wise? Do they even know you've contacted me?"

"Eugenia was aware we were trying to locate other family members—that's all. No one else has been apprised of the situation."

Not good news. It was going to be a shock to his father's wife, for sure. His half-brother's wife was an unknown.

"Now that you're here, I'll arrange for the reading of the will for a week from Thursday. I'll need to know where you're staying in case I need to get in touch while you're here. A phone number, as well."

Hunter gave Günter Jordan the information and then rose to leave.

"Do you think it appropriate I visit my half-brother in the hospital?"

Günter Jordan rose as well. "You are family. I'm sure they'll let you in—but he's in I.C.U. so visiting time is limited." He leaned over the desk and extended his hand. "If you don't mind me saying so, you are the spitting image of your father. You have the same sable eyes and dark hair. I'm assuming you get the darker skin tone from your mother's Hawaiian heritage."

Hunter paused, raised his eyebrows before accepting the lawyer's outstretched hand in farewell. His mother had never commented on his resemblance to his father. He had never given it a second thought, let alone a first thought.

"I see I have shocked you. I'm sorry. I doubt anyone will refute your paternity once they get a good look at your strong, dark Irish features. Let me know if the hospital staff gives you any trouble getting in to see Sebastian. I'll set them straight."

****

"What do you mean she is the one to decide whether or not my son lives? You can't be serious?" Eugenia's question was more of a screech.

Doctor Willson's expression didn't change, obviously used to such outbursts in circumstances where family members were asked to decide on a loved one's final life decisions without their knowledge.

Thankfully, the conversation took place outside Sebastian's room. Juelle didn't blame Eugenia for being upset. She didn't want to have to make the decision to pull life support, either. She sat in shock while her mother-in-law continued to pace and yell, her hands flying about in front of her, her heels clicking on the tiled floor, her face flushed, her eyes bulging, and her hair messed from running her hands through it for the last five minutes. She looked like a zombie, her makeup in shambles.

"My son is not ready to leave this world. You have no right to try to end his life by taking him off life support. I'll sue. Watch me."

"Mrs. McClintock. I understand your concern and sorrow." Dr. Willson intervened and stepped forward. "But believe me, your son's vital functions are shutting down. There has been no sign of movement in the past week. We have been monitoring him for two weeks now, and there is nothing more we can do. I am sorry." The doctor's face remained impassive as if he'd had to impart such news many times. "Unfortunately, Mrs. McClintock, the Living Will in our file states his wife, Juelle McClintock, has the unfortunate task of giving us permission to remove life support. I am sorry, but we will need her decision as soon as possible. Perhaps within the next twenty-four hours would be best."

"No! I won't have it. She is not going to be allowed to murder my son."

Eugenia stopped in front of the glass door outside Sebastian's room. With hands on her heart, she stared at her son. Tears streamed down her cheeks. Juelle had all she could do to hold back her own tears. Could she do it? Could she tell the doctors to let her husband go? And if she did, would it be murder, as Eugenia accused? She lowered her head and shut her eyes before her tears could fall. She fisted her hands and took several deep breaths, swallowed. God, she was tired of holding it all in.

She swung away from the scene in front of her, and headed for the door, only to be brought up short by a man standing there as if he'd been gob-struck. The man she'd seen at Mariner's the night before blocked her exit. Before she could ask why he was here, Eugenia's gasp drew her attention back to her mother-in-law. Clasping the back of a chair, the woman looked ready to pass out. Eugenia recovered so fast, Juelle wondered if she had imagined her mother-in-law's reaction.

"What the hell are you doing here? Get him out of here. *He! Is! Not! Family!*" Eugenia screeched.

Juelle did a double-take. If she considered Eugenia sounded like a banshee before, with her ear splitting shrieking, her tone now was so venomous it had everyone stopping in their tracks and staring in disbelief. The strange man was the first to recover. He walked into the enclosed room. Juelle recognized the astonishment in his pinched lips, raised eyebrows.

"I *am* family." His voice was calm, well-modulated, and confident. "Allow me to introduce myself—Hunter McClintock. I assume you know my father?"

Juelle's mouth dropped. She couldn't form a single sane word. Eugenia, however, had no trouble.

"Liar! Hunt McClintock's *only* son is lying in that bed." She stepped forward and pointed toward the I.C.U. cubicle, then reached back and braced herself against the chair once again for support. She leaned forward to emphasize her declaration. "I don't know who you are or what you hope to gain by coming here pretending to be Hunt's son," she jabbed her finger at him, "but you've wasted your time. Get out of here. *Now!*"

"Eugenia, please calm down. You're under a lot of stress. This can't be good for you." Juelle placed a comforting hand on her mother-in-law's shoulder. Eugenia shrugged it off.

"You can leave as well. You're nothing but a murderer."

"Excuse me, but your daughter-in-law is right, Mrs. McClintock." Dr. Willson approached and laid a comforting hand on Eugenia's shoulder. Eugenia didn't object to the doctor's touch. "Have a seat and I'll order one of the nurses to get something to calm you." He turned to the man standing in the doorway. "Mrs. McClintock has just learned there is nothing more we can do for her son. Your presence seems to have upset her further. Perhaps it would be best if you leave for now."

Hunter McClintock peered through the glass cubical at his half-brother, and then allowed the doctor to lead him out of the room.

If Hunter McClintock was not Hunt's son, he was a very, very close relative—he was the spitting image of the young Hunt McClintock displayed in a number of framed photos on Eugenia's fireplace mantel. No wonder he'd looked familiar when she'd seen him at Mariner's last night. Had Hunt been married before? Had a child? Where had this child been all these years? And did Eugenia know about him? If her reaction at seeing him was any indication, even if she did, she never expected to see him in Lobster Cove. And certainly not at Sebastian's deathbed. The poor woman didn't need another shock, she'd suffered enough already.

"I don't want to leave you here all alone, Eugenia. You need someone—"

"I'm not alone. I'm with my son."

Her mother-in-law's tone was despondent, and Juelle's heart ached for the woman. She might be hard to live with, and a force to be reckoned with, but it didn't mean she didn't have a heart—a heart that was breaking all over again.

Before she left, Juelle returned to Sebastian's bedside and squeezed his cold hand. How could she let them take him away from Eugenia? From their daughter, Makenzie. She didn't think she could.

****

Hunter shut the door as he exited the explosive confrontation he'd just walked in on. He'd heard enough. He hadn't expected anything less, but hadn't counted on it happening quite so soon after arriving in Lobster Cove. His half-brother's mother had stirred up a bee-hive, and his presence hadn't helped. It was a foregone conclusion she wasn't going to be happy that he'd been called to Lobster Cove for the reading of her husband's will. Günter Jordan should have warned her that he was coming—prepared the woman for the inevitable.

Hunter rested against the wall next to the window. What the hell was he doing here? Was it worth coming all this way only to be confronted by a mad woman? From the eighth-floor window, he had a partial view of the harbor over the top of the park trees. The usual calming effect of water slapping against a white sandy shore was nowhere to be seen. Various sailboats, bobbing along the harbor dock in the distance, held a familiar ring, and although a familiar scene at the marinas back home, the lack of tropical sandy shores failed to warm his heart. *Inheritance be dammed!* He had the strongest urge to pack up and go home. He wanted nothing from his estranged father. *Nothing!*

Should he go home, or stick it out to find out what developed? He was torn. And Sebastian's poor wife? A stunning, beautiful woman—her lush strawberry-blond hair, large sea-green eyes so woebegone looking as she faced her mother-in-law's tirade. He had the strangest and strongest urge to go to her and wrap her in his arms—comfort her. They hadn't been formally introduced, but he didn't need to know her name to see she not only grieved for her husband, but she was resolved to a fate of having to deal with a shrewish mother-in-law.

Hunter sighed, shifted, and ran his trembling

fingers though his hair. No way would he want the responsibility of having to end a spouse's life. Especially after being called a murderer. That alone must have stung. How the young wife could stand there and take such verbal abuse was beyond him. His chest ached just thinking of what she must be going through, about to lose her husband and having to deal with a callous mother-in-law. He shook his head.

Deciding to come back to visit his half-brother later, when the queen bee wasn't around, Hunter shoved away from the window and walked past the busy nurses station on his way out of the I.C.U. hospital wing. He needed to cool off. Might just as well see something of the area. A drive up around Acadia sounded like a good idea.

****

Juelle wanted to scream, but what good would it do? No way did she want to have to make the decision to unplug Sebastian's life support. However, it wasn't in anyone's interest to let Sebastian remain in such a state indefinitely. She recalled Eugenia's words and the wretched look on her face, and shuddered. If she didn't already feel guilty about having considered asking Sebastian for a divorce six months ago, Eugenia's accusations just clinched top spot on the guilt meter. Could her life get any more complicated?

She had twenty-four hours to make up her mind, to figure out how to make things right with Eugenia. But would her mother-in-law listen? She didn't look forward to the confrontation they were sure to have later. In the meantime, she had to compose herself and go pick up Makenzie so Katelyn could go to work.

Juelle pulled into Katelyn's drive just as her friend

wheeled Makenzie up the walk in an old fashioned baby carriage. She turned the ignition off in her Beetle, and got out of the car as Katelyn drew near.

"Shhh. The darling girl is napping. It's such a beautiful day, I wanted to get in a walk. How'd it go today?"

"You don't want to know," she sighed. She was past the crying stage. Her head throbbed, her shoulders weighed a ton, and she could sleep for a month of Sundays. She pocketed her keys and followed her friend through the gate to the backyard.

"You're looking more stressed today than usual. Come on. We'll have an iced tea and talk. Makenzie will be okay in the carriage under the shade tree."

"I don't know what I'd do without you. You've been a godsend since Sebastian's accident. I know I should be looking for a fulltime babysitter soon, or even a daycare..."

"Don't worry about it. I'm glad to help out. Sit and relax while I get our tea."

Juelle strode to the carriage, bent over her daughter, and brushed a wispy red curl aside, then kissed Makenzie on her smooth cheek. Her heart swelled with happiness. No matter the outcome with Sebastian, she would ever be grateful he'd given her this adorable babe. Could she live with Makenzie thinking she'd killed Sebastian? Would her daughter grow to hate her?

Juelle let out a heavy sigh and sat down in one of the white wicker chairs arranged around a round table. Life just wasn't fair sometimes.

"Here we are. My mom sent over one of her famous wild blueberry pies, so I cut us each a large piece. Something tells me you need a pick-me-up."

"Thanks. She does make the best pies in Lobster Cove." Juelle wasn't sure she could eat any, but she didn't want to hurt her friend's, or Mrs. Sullivan's feelings.

"Okay, so, tell me what has you so upset. Besides Sebastian."

"Are you sure you want to hear this?" She took a long sip of tea and forked a portion of the pie into her mouth, stalling for time so she could pull herself together.

"You need to finally get it all out. And I have plenty of time today. So, spill."

"The short version? I have twenty-four hours to decide whether to pull Sebastian's life support before they take further action to keep him hooked up indefinitely even though they aren't holding out much hope of him ever coming out of it, and Eugenia freaked out and called me a murderer. Oh, and the man we spotted at Mariner's last night—the one everyone hadn't been able to stop looking at, or gossiping about? The gorgeous hunk who looked familiar? He's Sebastian's half-brother—he's Hunt's son from another marriage. His name is—ready for this? Hunter McClintock."

"No! Really? You've got to be kidding. What are the odds? What was Eugenia's reaction?"

"Called him a liar and told him to get out. She lost it—looked as if she was about to have a heart attack. There was no consoling her. The doctor asked him to leave, and then ordered the nurse to administer something to calm her down."

"Did it help?"

"I didn't stay to find out. I was banished, as well. What am I going to do, Katelyn? How can I tell the doctors to take Sebastian off life support? It's bad enough I contemplated asking the guy for a divorce, but to end his life? I may not have strong feelings for Sebastian any longer, but I don't want to be responsible for killing him."

"First off, you aren't going to be killing him. He set sail in a company trawler of his own free will knowing full well there was a storm brewing. You did not cause the accident." Katelyn sipped her tea and took another bite of pie. "A wave lifted the boat, it capsized, and he hit his head going overboard."

"I know what happened." Juelle hung her head. She'd lived the details over and over, again and again— while she sat at his side in the hospital, when she laid down at night in bed, when Eugenia bemoaned the fact every day. Juelle had done nothing but try and figure out why she suffered from a guilt that wasn't hers. "I know you're right, but that doesn't make it any easier to have to decide on whether someone is to live or die."

"Have you talked to your parents?"

"They've moved on to another missionary location somewhere in the back of beyond in Africa. They won't be back for another six months. They're in some remote area that doesn't have modern communications." It wasn't unusual for her parents to be gone for long periods of time, they were dedicated to their missionary work. And she loved them for it, even though they hadn't been your normal "raising kids" type of parents. They loved her and were very attentive when they were home.

"I'm the last person to give advice," Katelyn broke

into Juelle's musings. "But you have to start thinking about yourself—and your daughter. You need to look for an apartment or a house. You need to get out from under Eugenia's thumb."

"How can I leave her at a time like this? She's all alone."

"There will always be something to keep you there. You need to make the break."

"Sebastian…"

Katelyn leaned across the table and pointed her finger at Juelle, reminding her of Eugenia. She couldn't help but smile.

"Sebastian hasn't been a decent husband since Makenzie was born and you know it. You've spent more time with me than you have with him. You can't let his death nail you to Eugenia's side the rest of your life."

Juelle's smile faded, she rested her elbows on the table. "You're right. Although to be fair, he had to take over for his father after Hunt died and worked overtime a lot. The fishermen in the community depend on his business for their employment."

"Honey, you're my best friend, but I've got to say, Sebastian is more like his mother than Hunt, and he was only ever concerned about himself. Face facts, it was never going to get better between the two of you as long as you lived under Eugenia's roof."

"I know you're trying to help, and I appreciate it. I have twenty-four hours—the clock is ticking, and I'm so sick to my stomach I don't know what to do."

"Simple. Tell Eugenia she can be the one to make the decision. Lets you off the hook. Puts the guilt back in her court."

"If I do, she'll let Sebastian lay in that bed until the day she dies."

"You could be right. But then, you wouldn't be the one carrying the decision on your shoulders for the rest of your life. Sounds to me as if you've made up your mind."

"No. I can't do it. I would hate myself. Makenzie would grow up without her father. She'd hate me for causing her father's death. No. No way. I couldn't live with her hating me the rest of her life."

Chapter Four

Eugenia entered Günter Jordan's law office. Jordan and Jordan, Attorney at Law, had taken over the old Maynard home after his partner, his father Fredrick, died five years ago. She didn't bother knocking, nor considered it necessary to stop at the receptionist's desk. Günter expected her.

"Mrs. McClintock, if you'll wait here, I'll let Mr. Jordan know you've arrived," Günter Jordan's receptionist said, holding her hand up.

As if the woman could stop her. Still, Carrie Saunders rose to let her boss know she was there, but Eugenia stopped her before Carrie made it around the desk.

"Not necessary, my dear. I'll show myself in. He's expecting me."

Eugenia wasted no time. She veered right and walked down the hall, turned the handle on Günter's office door, and walked in before the receptionist could pick up the intercom to inform him she was on her way.

"Eugenia!" Günter jumped from behind his own desk, waving at Carrie, dismissing her with a shake of his head. "Have a seat. What can I do for you?" He circled back to his chair, waited for her to have a seat, and then sat.

Eugenia didn't give him a chance to continue with pleasantries.

"What the hell is going on, Günter? Who was that man who showed up at my son's bedside? If you tell me he is Hunt's son and you contacted him, I'm going to sue the pants off of you—friend or no friend—he doesn't belong here."

"Don't threaten me, Eugenia. Your financial weight has no effect on me, or this company. I am doing my job. Sue me if you wish, but it won't do you any good."

His half grin ticked her off. He was right, but it still stung.

"What the hell is he doing here? Just what is in Hunt's will? What are you keeping from me? He was my husband, I have a right to know."

"All in good time, all in good time. Take a deep breath and relax a minute, and then tell me what is it that really has you so upset this time."

Eugenia huffed. The gall of the man thinking she was upset over nothing. Had the man never lost a loved one, and then another so soon? Did he know what it was like to be tossed from one foster home to another? To feel so alone? He might be a good friend, but this was business. She was tired of waiting around to put an end to the worry over Hunt's last requests. She needed to put Hunt to rest. And to put the employees' minds at ease over the status of the family lobster business. To move on with her own life and concentrate on her son's health crisis.

"What is to become of the business? My son incapacitated at the moment, and Coleman Baker is acting on Sebastian's behalf until he recuperates and gets back on his feet."

"Now, Eugenia, you know as well as I the doctors

are not holding out much hope for Sebastian's recovery. In fact, I understand your daughter-in-law has twenty-four hours to decide whether or not to pull the plug on his life support. It might not be my place to say so, but it's probably for the best. The company, although a wealthy one at the moment, cannot continue to cough up the expenses needed to maintain life support indefinitely, and your insurance won't cover it forever, either. So, unless you want to go bankrupt and lose everything you own, including your home, and whatever you might inherit from Hunt, you might want to think about the consequences of your actions."

Eugenia stared at her clenched hands in her lap, her lips pinched tight, she shut her eyes and contemplated Günter's words. He made sense. Still, it was her son they were talking about as if he was some unknown person and her heart wasn't involved.

"Look, Eugenia, we've been friends a long time. I know how difficult this is for you, but you have to look ahead. What kind of life will Sebastian have? I'm talking quality of life? And what about you? You are young enough to get past all of this and get on with your own life. Have a life of your own again. You have a daughter-in-law and a granddaughter—Sebastian's daughter…"

Eugenia remained quiet. Günter wasn't telling her anything she hadn't already told herself. Still, the fear of being alone, having everything taken from her was worth fighting for. Wasn't it?

"If you are such a good friend, why won't you do me this one favor and tell me what this man is doing here—what's in Hunt's will?"

"Aw, Eugenia, you know I can't do that. I have to

follow protocol. Just know Hunt has made sure you will be well taken care of for the rest of your life. I've set the date for the reading of the will. Soon. It will all be over soon. Remember, I'll be here if you need me."

It had been forever since she'd shed a tear on her own behalf, but they threatened now. She had to leave before Günter found out what a fraud she really was.

****

Juelle pulled her car up to the three-car garage on the side of the massive Victorian style mansion overlooking the harbor and Frenchman Bay. She hit the button to open the end door and drove her car inside. She sat for a moment, anticipating the conversation she was about to have with her mother-in-law. It was never easy talking to Eugenia. Taking a deep breath, she got out and opened the back car door and lifted Makenzie out of her car seat, and then entered the house through the side door to the McClintock Estate.

The house was a sprawling, two-story mansion-type home with professionally manicured lawns. The house had been in the family for many generations. It sat high on a cliff overlooking the harbor. She kicked off her flats, headed for the parlor, and settled Makenzie in the playpen next to the window, making sure her daughter's favorite cloth picture book, plastic alphabet blocks, and Tilley the teddy bear were tucked in the corners. She kissed the top of her daughter's head, ruffled her curls, and went to the kitchen to warm a bottle of milk. When she returned, Makenzie was holding on to the edge of the padded playpen bouncing up and down. Her girl would be striking out on her own without the aid of an adult's hand before long. Her toothless smile was Juelle's undoing. She couldn't resist a chuckle, which encouraged her daughter to laugh along with her.

"Ma-ma." Makenzie clapped and reached for the bottle with anxious hands.

"Here you go, pumpkin. Something warm to drink."

Makenzie latched on to the bottle, plunked down on her fanny, and started sucking. Juelle waited until Makenzie finished and was settled before she went in search of her mother-in-law. It was now or never—she had to get this conversation over with before she chickened out. The sooner she did, the sooner she could make peace with herself.

She found Eugenia in the atrium, a rather small room for such a big estate. Juelle found it to be a cozy and relaxing place for wishful thinking and day dreams. Would the surrounding plants and miniature waterfall against the outside wall have a calming effect on Eugenia so she would be in a receptive frame of mind? One could only hope.

"Eugenia, may I have a word, please?"

Eugenia jumped, turned toward her, and frowned. The startled look wasn't encouraging. Nor welcoming. This was going to be harder than she'd anticipated, and she hadn't anticipated a warm welcome to begin with. She took a deep reassuring breath and stepped forward when Eugenia spoke.

"I was just contemplating your dire dilemma, my dear. It hasn't escaped me that you and Sebastian haven't been the most enamored of each other since Makenzie was born. I've often wondered if in fact she was Sebastian's child."

"*Excuse me!*" Juelle jumped back in shock, her

hands clenched against her chest, her head shot back. She wasn't sure what to make of this turn of events. She definitely hadn't anticipated this. "Are you implying what I think you're implying? Oh, my, God. How could you?" Where was this woman coming up with such hogwash? "Of course Makenzie is Sebastian's daughter. Why would I lie about Sebastian being her father?"

"You've got to admit, your daughter looks more like you than she does Sebastian."

Juelle's hackles rose to fever pitch. The nerve of this woman accusing her of being unfaithful.

"*Yes! Eugenia. Makenzie is Sebastian's child.*" Juelle's teeth gnashed, she bit her lower lip to keep her temper from overflowing. "Why would you even think otherwise?"

"These things happen. We are a wealthy family and you will more than likely gain a portion of the McClintock wealth if you pull the plug on my son. Am I right?"

"*Enough, Eugenia!* I've put up with a lot from you and your son over the last two years, and while I try to understand your point of view in order to keep the peace, I've done nothing but bang my head against the wall to no avail. What the hell have I ever done to you?"

"Don't you use that tone with me."

"*Eugenia—*"

"You really want to know?" She stood to face Juelle, her hands on her hips, her face scrunched up as if she'd bit into a sour lemon.

Juelle held her tongue and waited. The woman made her crazy.

"You honestly want to know? I'll tell you—you aren't good enough for my son. You are only after his money."

Her mother-in-law had always exuded strong negative emotions toward her—they weren't hard to miss. But she had never verbalized her true feelings— face to face. And they stung. She'd had no idea this was why Eugenia was so hard on her. Marrying Sebastian had nothing to do with his wealth. In fact, he had never mentioned the family was wealthy until after he'd asked her to marry him. And not having lived in Lobster Cove or the State of Maine until they were married, Juelle had no way of knowing. The woman might just as well have slapped her silly, the shock reverberated clear to her toes.

"You've been trying to take my son away from me—make him move out of the only true home he's ever known. You've come in here, taken over his life, and turned him against me. You want to leave? Go out on your own so bad? Then leave. Get out. You have my permission."

Juelle's head shot back, her eyes wide, she stared, open mouthed, at her mother-in-law. She hadn't seen that one coming. Wasn't prepared.

It only took ten seconds to regain her sanity. Despite the fact she'd just been labeled a gold-digger, there was the more urgent issue of Sebastian's life support. She squared her shoulders and dug in.

"Eugenia. We have to discuss the situation in regards to Sebastian. I think you should be the one to decide. I know you've lost so much already. I don't want to cause you any more heartache."

Eugenia sat back down—actually plunked down as

if her legs could no longer support her. If she didn't know any better, she'd just taken the wind right out of Eugenia's sail. It was a first. She'd been to too many committee meetings with the woman, and Eugenia always…, always came out on top—always in control and having the last word. And although besting Eugenia now should have made her ecstatic, it didn't.

"I'll contact the doctors and let them know the decision is yours."

Eugenia remained silent. Juelle waited several long seconds, contemplating her mother-in-law's next words, when it finally dawned on her that her mother-in-law had actually told her to leave, to move out of the house. Now that she had permission, she didn't think it a good idea. Eugenia was not in a mentally stable condition to be alone. Still…she would seriously work on finding a place of her own. She'd be ready when the time came.

When Eugenia remained silent, Juelle determined it was time to leave her mother-in-law to her own thoughts—to reflect on her decision in regards to Sebastian. It was time to pick up Makenzie and go cool off.

"I'm taking Makenzie to the park. Don't hold dinner for us tonight."

Juelle made it as far as the door before Eugenia stopped her.

"Don't bother calling the hospital," she spoke between tight lips. "You think I don't know what you're trying to do? Make me responsible for my own son's death?"

Juelle couldn't listen to another word. She stiffened her shoulders, quietly shut the door behind her, and sucked in a deep breath as she propped herself up against the wall. She had to shake off the bad vibes before she picked up her daughter. She ran up the stairs to her room, restocked the diaper bag, and grabbed her purse off the dresser. Her sweater lay on the bed. She snatched it, and then ran back down the stairs to the parlor. She scooped up Makenzie, a few of her toys, including Tilley, and headed out the door.

Really. Could life get any more complicated?

****

Hunter sat on the blue Adirondack chair outside his motel room door. The sun had faded, although there was still much daylight and the Maine summer air was temperate and refreshing. The breeze off the bay was filled with the scent of the sea—the docks, the marine life, and the faint aroma of enticing foods from the various diners and family cookouts. His stomach rumbled, reminding him of the first-class meal he'd enjoyed the previous evening at Mariner's Fish Fry. It was a bit early to eat right now, so he kicked his feet up against the chair's matching foot stool, steepled his fingers in his lap, tilted back in the deck chair, and shut his eyes.

Big mistake. Juelle McClintock's image popped up front and center. A warm feeling hit his gut and radiated to regions of his body it had no business radiating to. The last thing he needed in Lobster Cove was to have his manly parts go crazy for anyone, especially his half-brother's wife—a very enticing woman with all her womanly parts in the right place. He rubbed his hands over his face as if that would wash away his uncalled for thoughts and his troubles. It didn't do a thing to ease his anger.

Half-brother! How the hell was he supposed to feel about a half-brother he never knew he had, and was too late to get to know. His lips tightened. He swung his legs off the stool—his feet hit the porch at the same time his eyes shot open. He sat up ramrod straight. He wasn't angry at Sebastian—how could he be? The man probably didn't know he existed either. No, his anger was targeted at his father—a father he'd never laid eyes on. A father who left him and his mother behind to come back to Maine to raise another family. He wished the S.O.B. was still alive so he could finally confront him.

Hell, he was angry at himself for not having the balls to confront his father years ago—while the man was still alive.

Hunter jumped over the railing and the boxwood bushes, and stormed down the street, mindless of where he was heading. Traffic was light on Main Street, a few bicyclers peddled by and waved. Hunter passively waved back, surprised when they turned their heads in his direction as they kept going. Two older men, back from fishing the docks, passed him on the sidewalk, smiled and gave a guttural 'ayah' with heads turned toward him as they continued walking. He nodded in return. People in Maine were certainly a friendly bunch.

After the first three blocks his strides slowed, his breathing back to normal. Why the hell had he let his mother talk him into coming to Lobster Cove? What made her think that if there was nothing here for her, there'd be anything here for him?

He kept walking until he arrived at a park across from the harbor. A black marble statue of a fisherman looking out to sea stood next to the Captain's Library across the way. A playground was situated to the left, where he spotted Sebastian's wife pushing a small child on the swing set. *Shit*. The woman had a kid. This whole deal must be even harder on her having the responsibility of soon becoming a single mom.

His gut twisted. Torn between going over and offering his sincere apology for disrupting her and her mother-in law's heated conversation at the hospital, and walking away, he stepped off the sidewalk and headed in her direction before he changed his mind. Halfway across the grass, however, he paused. Was he about to make her situation worse? The woman didn't need any more trouble than she apparently had dealing with a cranky mother-in-law from hell.

She turned and spotted him as he was about to change his mind and head back to his motel. Their eyes locked. The smile on her face froze. Hunter pressed forward, his awareness of her as a woman radiated deep into his core. He should have turned around—backed off and fled for cover. Their gazes never faltered, and suddenly he was at her side.

"I was walking by and saw you—wanted to apologize for intruding and creating a scene with your mother-in-law at the hospital. I hadn't expected to meet the family at the hospital—just wanted to meet my half-brother. I'm sorry if my presence caused you any further pain. It wasn't my intent."

The woman was even more beautiful up close. Oh, God. Her sea-green eyes looked tired, worried. Sad. He wanted to wrap her in his arms—something that was becoming all too familiar a feeling when he was near her.

"No need to apologize. Eugenia isn't an easy

person to deal with at the best of times. Right or wrong, she's pretty forthright. And intimidating."

Her voice floated on the air and Hunter had to shake himself to snap out of the sappy person he was starting to become. She wasn't his responsibility just because Sebastian was his half-brother.

She continued to swing the child in short, gentle strokes—a tiny girl the replica of her mother—strawberry-blonde hair, dazzling sea-green eyes—all smiles as she kicked her feet in the air having the time of her life. The girl was going to drive the boys crazy when she hit high school. It brought a smile to his lips. He'd love to have been around when Juelle had been a teenager.

"Is this your daughter?" He extended his hand, moved into her space—her clean, fruity scent filled his senses and he almost lost his voice.

"Yes. This is Makenzie. And I'm Juelle. Sorry, we met under tense circumstances and we weren't formally introduced yesterday."

Her hand in his was a mistake. What the hell was the matter with him? He had to stop this…what-ever-the-hell 'this' was. She belonged to Sebastian. She might just as well be wearing a sign that said Hands Off.

"Understandable. Again, I'm sorry my presence caused such a stir."

Her name was a perfect fit. Anyone who put up with a queen bee such as Eugenia McClintock had to be a jewel. Or an angel.

"If it helps, I don't plan to be in the area long. I'll be out of everyone's hair as soon as my father's will is read next week."

"I'm sorry about Eugenia's outburst, but you do resemble Hunt. A lot." She continued to push her daughter in the swing. A devilish, toothless smile lit the tot's face. "I suspect that's why Eugenia was so upset when you walked into the hospital room. I have a feeling she was aware Hunt had another son. The shock on her face when she spotted you said it all. Neither she nor Hunt ever mentioned another child, let alone another marriage—at least not to me."

Hunter's anger swelled inside his gut. He held it in. This beautiful jewel of a woman standing in front of him was an innocent bystander. Kind of like him. Except he'd been an innocent bystander for the last twenty-eight years.

"Doesn't surprise me. He never tried to contact my mother, or me, after he left her behind in Oahu."

"You live in Hawaii? That would account for your tan."

He liked the glimmer in her eyes and the smile that lit up her lovely face.

"Actually, my mother is part Hawaiian, so it's not all tan. Although, I do spend a lot of time in the sun and surf. My mother and I own the Lani Aloha Travel Agency—there's a lot of perks escorting tourists around the islands."

"I've always wanted to spend a couple of weeks on the islands, especially in the winter months. It gets pretty chilly around here, so close to the ocean."

"Let me know if you get serious about a visit. I can arrange it."

Makenzie started to fuss, obviously she'd had enough of the swing. Used to being around all his many cousins and their kids, he was about to go to the tyke's aid, but held back. Instead, he stepped aside to let Juelle deal with her daughter. He was mesmerized by the scene enfolding in front of him. The curly top, red haired babe snuggled against her mother's body, wrapping her arms around Juelle's slender neck. Hunter's heart raced. He had to look out at the early evening water on the harbor to rein in his libido.

The tide was on its way out for the evening—his sanity with it. How could he be jealous of a baby wrapping her arms around a mother's neck? A woman he'd just met? A woman who belonged to another man—his half-brother? Shit. There must be some unexplained enchantment floating around in the Maine coastal breeze to whisper such images causing his libido and mind to go bonkers. And turn to mush. He shook his head, looked back at the mother and daughter. Another warm tug hit his chest. A good thing he wouldn't be in the area long. Once Hunt McClintock's will was read, he was out of here.

Chapter Five

Juelle was thankful for Makenzie's interruption. She lifted her daughter from the swing and cuddled her distraught child. Hunter's nearness had her stomach fluttering and her temperature rising. Was Eugenia right? Was Hunter a scam artist who had come to collect? Somehow it didn't fit. He didn't seem the sleazy sort. And he had backed off at the hospital without making a fuss.

The evening breeze off the harbor was deliciously cooling. The man was very striking—tall, tanned, his thick sable hair hung over his forehead and curled around his ears. Even his demeanor was hard to resist at first meeting. She had no business letting this man affect her like this—she was married, had a child. Her insides hummed at his closeness. She needed to get a grip. Not get tangled up with this man whom she didn't know.

She bent over, put Makenzie down on the ground, and then hung on to her daughter's hand, the tiny fingers clasped onto hers as the toddler wobbled over the grass to the small slide. She hadn't expected Hunter to follow them, but he did.

"Here, let me hold her up on top of the slide and you can catch her at the bottom."

He reached for Makenzie, but her daughter turned back in fear and grabbed on to her pant legs, as she'd done every time when meeting strangers. Juelle lifted her daughter into her arms.

"I'm sorry, she tends to be a bit shy around people she's never met. But thanks for offering to help."

"I'm good with kids. I swear. I have a whole bunch of cousins at home who love me."

"Give her time. I'm sure she'll come around."

Juelle placed her carefully on the top platform and kept a secure hold on her as she helped Makenzie slide to the bottom.

"Here, let me try it. Maybe if you hand her to me and tell her it's okay."

Together they walked to the platform. Juelle made sure Makenzie was on the side next to Hunter as they walked.

"Makenzie, this here is Hunter. He's your daddy's brother. He's going to hold you on top of the slide and I'll be right on the bottom to catch you."

Makenzie held back

"Hi. Makenzie. Do you want to go for a ride on the slide?"

Juelle was pleased when her daughter accepted Hunter's invitation. He kept her secure in his hold, waiting for Juelle to get into position at the bottom. The slide was deep enough so Makenzie, and other young children, wouldn't slip off the edges, and the length of the ride was short. Juelle squatted down ready to catch Makenzie before she hit the ground.

"Ready?" Hunter asked, as he wiggled Makenzie around the waist, making her chortle before he let go.

Makenzie giggled the entire way down the slide and clapped her hands when Juelle lifted her off at the end of the ride and twirled her around in the air, her legs kicking out behind her in joy.

"More. More," Makenzie shouted.

"Thanks for your help." Juelle smiled at Hunter. "I can take it from here. I'm sure you have other things to do."

"Are you kidding? This is the most fun I've had since I arrived in Maine. But don't you have somewhere else to be?"

"Not tonight. Tonight Makenzie and I are having a picnic here in the park." She smiled, hopefully hiding her anxiety over Eugenia's reactions to their earlier conversation. If she played her cards right, Eugenia will have retired to her room when she returned to the estate for the evening, and she wouldn't have to face another confrontation. She couldn't help the sigh that escaped.

"That sigh was pretty telling." Hunter looked at her, his eyebrows raised and Juelle's heart picked up a wicked beat. "It must be hard to deal with an unpleasant mother-in-law while having to accept the fact your husband is laying in the hospital dying."

"It's complicated. Like you said, this will all be over soon. In the meantime, like everyone else, we have to take it one day at a time. But with Makenzie, I have to look forward."

"If you need a shoulder, I'm available."

His arms were definitely big and sturdy looking. She wished he hadn't mentioned his shoulder—it was as if he'd read her mind. His caring look had wanting to run into his arms. She could use a comforting shoulder to lean on right about now. But Hunter McClintock's shoulder was off limits.

"If you want to confide in me, know it will go back with me to Oahu. Your secrets will be safe. I promise."

"That's kind of you, but I'm fine. Really."

Juelle spread a blanket down on the grass. She had planned on an impromptu picnic when she walked out on Eugenia, and had called ahead to Mariner's Fish Fry to ask Mrs. Sullivan to prepare a picnic for one. The restaurant offered bag lunches for the many hikers who came through to enjoy the island's great outdoors. It had been ready when she'd stopped in to pick it up before heading to the park.

"You can't keep things bottled up inside." He stood at the edge of the blanket, hands in his slacks' pockets, looking out over the park. "It will eat you alive. I know just how toxic it can become. I never met my father, and now he's dead, and there is no chance of that ever happening."

"I'm sorry. It must have been hard for you, never knowing him." Had she detected a slight catch in his voice? She wasn't sure what to say. Was he telling her this in an effort to put her mind at ease, or get it out his own system now that he was here in Lobster Cove?

"I told myself it didn't bother me, but I was only kidding myself. It didn't faze me much until I was in fifth grade—sports—all boys want to share sports with their fathers."

"I'm sorry he wasn't there for you." She looked up at him. Was he telling the truth? Or was Eugenia? He did resemble her father-in-law. She didn't know what to believe.

He blinked, and then looked her in the eyes.

"You're too generous. Here I am, trying to console you, and you're more sympathetic about my problems which you don't need to worry about. You have enough on your own plate. I'm sorry."

"They are sort of connected…"

She pulled a sweater out of the diaper bag and wrapped it around Makenzie, then reached in for a box of animal crackers. Makenzie's hands shot out, anxious for Juelle to open the box.

"Care to join us for an impromptu picnic?" She heard herself invite him, not sure why, or if it was wise. "Mrs. Sullivan always packs too much, and I wouldn't want it to go to waste."

To her amazement, he sat cross-legged on the edge of the blanket, picked up one of the crackers Makenzie dropped, and handed it to her. Her daughter threw her head back, smiled up at Hunter, and then clutched the cracker and shoved it into her mouth. Apparently, she was now familiar enough with Hunter that she was no longer afraid of him. The ride down the slide did the trick.

"She's a beautiful child. Looks just like you."

Juelle didn't know how to respond. Reminded of what Eugenia had accused her of not too long ago, she bowed her head to hide the resentment she'd suffered at her mother-in-law's words. Had Hunter visited his half-brother after they left? Had he noticed Makenzie didn't look much like her father? Would he think Makenzie wasn't Sebastian's? Did it matter?

"Thank you. There's chicken salad sandwiches and blueberry muffins enough for an army. Help yourself."

Juelle uncovered the plastic container with the sandwiches and the plastic wrap with the muffins and held them out to him. He reached in, withdrew a blueberry muffin, and bit into it.

"Mmmm. Delicious. Tastes homemade."

"They are. Dawn Sullivan bakes them daily.

There's ice tea in the thermos. I don't mind sharing."

Hunter helped himself to one of the sandwiches and didn't hesitate to dig in.

"You'll have to let me repay the favor while I'm in town—take you to lunch."

Sandwich halfway to her mouth, Juelle sighed, put her sandwich down, and shook her head. "We'll see. Sebastian is…"

He raised his left brow above an inquisitive eye, waiting for her to continue.

"It's complicated. I'm not sure that would be a good idea. I've had a lot on my mind lately, but thanks for the invitation."

"I did overhear what the doctor said in regard to Sebastian's life support. Have you made a decision yet?" He shook his head and looked away. "Sorry, that was insensitive of me. I didn't mean to upset you again. Forget I asked."

"No, no, that's okay. I haven't made a decision, yet." She heard her own voice crack, but still couldn't get the notion that he was only there to collect from the estate out of her mind. "In fact, I told Eugenia she should be the one to make the decision. I thought I was doing the right thing." She handed Makenzie a small bottle of milk.

"How did that go?"

"About a well as expected. She accused me of shifting the blame for ending Sebastian's life on to her shoulders so I wouldn't feel guilty."

"The witch."

Juelle's laugh sounded more like a gasp. She concurred with his description, but kept her opinion to herself. She liked his lopsided grin—her insides melted.

"What? Don't tell me you think she's right? I've only met the woman once, but I certainly don't want to be on the receiving end of another one of her tirades, not that I couldn't handle it. But there is usually no wining when someone has a bee in their bonnet."

She didn't tell him the rest. That Eugenia had told her to leave, to get out of the house. As much as she was happy to comply, she had nowhere to go at the moment. She made a half-hearted attempt to eat her sandwich. As delicious as it was, she no longer had any desire for food. Besides, she was sure once Eugenia settled down, she'd change her mind and find some trumped up reason for her to remain at the McClintock Estate with Makenzie.

"I'm sorry. I should go. I've imposed enough as it is." He swiped the napkin across his mouth.

Juelle couldn't take her eyes off his lips. They were full, rather defined for a man's. She figured whoever was on the receiving end of one of his kisses would have no trouble knowing she'd been thoroughly kissed. He probably had scores of beach beauties standing in line back home. She wondered if he had a girlfriend back home—she noticed he wasn't wearing a ring.

"Thanks for sharing."

She shook her thoughts away as he stood, ready to leave. What was the matter with her? She was a married woman for God's sake. Her husband was lying in the hospital at death's door. She stood, her hands hanging at her sides, unsure of how to respond to this man.

"If you need anything, anything at all, give me a call." He handed her a card with his cell number on it, and then leaned down and rubbed his large, muscular hand over the top of Makenzie's curls, giving them a muss. Makenzie giggled.

Juelle grasped the card as if it was her link to life and looked down at it. Next to the palm trees was his name—Hunter McClintock, Lani Aloha Travel Agency, and below that was his cell number in bold letters in the center. She'd give anything this very minute to be swept away to a warm tropical island and be able to leave all her troubles behind.

Before she could respond, he clasped her upper arms, his touch gentle, and stepped forward, pulling her forward into his space. Dazed, she wondered if he was about to kiss her. Her heart fluttered. She held her breath. Did she want him to? Inches taller than herself, he placed his warm lips on her forehead, and wrapped his arm around her, her own hands still dangling at her sides, and then gave her a gentle but all-encompassing hug.

"Anything," he whispered. "Just call."

Juelle shut her eyes. When she opened them, he was walking across the lawn. Shoulders slumped, she sat back down. Makenzie tugged on Tilley, giving her teddy bear hugs and slobbery smooches. Juelle opened a juice box and exchanged the bear for the drink, and then proceeded to finish feeding her daughter. She packed the rest of the baby food back in her bag, and then dealt with the remainder of the picnic items before moving Makenzie to the grass and folding the blanket. Makenzie rolled on her stomach and plucked at the grass. Juelle's cell phone rang as she was about to pick Makenzie back up and head to the car. She propped her wiggly daughter on her hip, dumped everything back on the ground, and pulled her cell from her side pocket. She checked the number. The hospital. What the hell had Eugenia done now?

"Mrs. McClintock. You need to come to the hospital as soon as possible."

"Is it Sebastian? Oh, my God. What's happened?"

"His mother is already here. You need to come at once."

Juelle's mind went blank. Her legs gave out and she sat down on the lawn. She let Makenzie crawl onto the grass.

"It will take me a few minutes to get there. I'll need to find a babysitter for my daughter. I'll be there as soon as I can."

She hung up, and with shaking fingers, dialed Katelyn. It took several rings before her friend picked up.

"What's up? How'd it go with Eugenia?"

"Oh, Katelyn, I don't have time to chat right now. The hospital just called. I have to get there as soon as possible. I don't know what's going on, but Eugenia is already there. Do you think you can take Makenzie for a few hours?"

"Of course. Save time. I'll meet you at the hospital and pick her up there."

Juelle hung up, gathered Makenzie and the picnic stuff in her arms, and make a mad dash for her car. She had Makenzie in the car seat, things stowed, and the key turned in the ignition in minutes. She didn't have far to drive to the hospital, but her heart raced, her throat dry. Should she call Hunter, let him know…what? What could she say? She didn't even know what was going on. Was Eugenia right? Was Hunter really not Hunt's long-lost son? Would Hunter even care?

Katelyn was waiting in the hospital parking lot when Juelle pulled in.

"Go. I'll transfer our darling girl into my own car while you go in. Don't worry about a thing. I'm stopping back at the diner before going home to let the folks know I won't be in right away. You can pick her up at the house when you're done here. No rush."

"Thanks, Katelyn. You're the best." She gave her daughter a kiss, her friend a hug, and then dashed into the hospital.

Eugenia waited outside Sebastian's I.C.U. room.

"He's gone," she wailed. "My son is gone."

Juelle ran to her side. "Did you have them remove life support?"

"Of course I didn't. How could I? Did you? Did you call them? Did you murder my son?"

Juelle stopped in her tracks and stepped back in shock.

"Mrs. McClintock." One of Sebastian's doctors Juelle had met over the past two weeks, but couldn't for the life of her remember his name at the moment, stepped between them. "I'm sorry, Mr. McClintock had a massive stroke a half hour ago. No one called to give orders to remove life support." He looked from one to the other. "It wasn't necessary. His vital organs shut down. I'm sorry for your loss. I'll have someone help you with the necessary details. You can both go in now, if you wish. Take your time. Stay as long as you want."

Once the doctor left, Juelle didn't quite know what to do first. Wanting to console Eugenia, drained from the stress over the past two weeks, and having the decision taken out of her hands, she leaned against the wall and prayed for strength.

"I'm so sorry, Eugenia. And I'm sorry for the things I said earlier today."

"Don't think this is going to change a thing. If you think you're going to gain from this, think again. As long as I have a breath left in me there will be nothing here for you. You won't get a dime."

With that, her mother-in-law swung around and marched across the room and knelt beside her son's deathbed. Juelle walked to the glass enclosure and touched the window.

"Goodbye, Sebastian," she whispered. "I hope you are at peace and in a better place."

A single tear trickled down her cheek. She wiped it away, took another moment, then left. There was nothing more to be done here. In any case, there was nothing Eugenia would allow.

Juelle sat in her car in the half empty parking lot, eyes closed, head resting on the back of the seat. What to do? Where did she go from here? She wanted to call her mother, but the only way to contact her parents was by mental telepathy. She wasn't ready to talk to Katelyn—her friend would analyze the situation to death and she wasn't in the mood. Should she call Hunter? Tell him Sebastian had died? She pulled his card out of her purse and rubbed her thumb over the front of the raised palm tree fronds...

And dialed his number.

****

For the first time in his adult life, Hunter was completely helpless. He wanted to go to Juelle, comfort her. She needed someone to be by her side, and he knew it sure as hell wasn't going to be her mother-in-law consoling her. The old battle-axe was probably blaming her for Sebastian's death, tearing up the hospital and ready to sue everyone in sight. His heart went out to her, but there wasn't a damn thing he could do about it at the moment. His presence would fire up a storm, and Juelle didn't need any more stress in her life. The best thing he could do for her was stay away. Let things run its course.

He shoved his cell back in its holder and strode to the end of the pier and didn't stop until he reached the very end. He stood, hands in pockets, and looked out over the water at the many sailboats, yachts, kayakers, fishermen, and lovers walking hand in hand along the rounded shore line of the harbor. He needed to talk to someone. Someone who would understand his position. He'd been within days of meeting a half-brother, face to face, and even he was dead. Just like his father. Although his buddies back home would be understanding, and several of their female friends would love to comfort him, he wasn't up to being pacified. He thought about calling his mother, but he didn't want to upset her long distance.

God, he could use a drink. There had to be a bar around this town somewhere. Hadn't he seen a sign advertising a local wine bar that had a coffee shop, too? He certainly didn't need coffee to keep him awake, but hopefully, there would be one within walking distance of his motel. He hung his head, turned, and headed back down the pier.

He spotted Merlots Wine Bar up ahead. It was open, but he decided against drinking away his problems. He knew it would only lead to more heartache—regrets. And right now he needed a sober brain if he was going to get through the next few days.

Chapter Six

Thick Maine fog swirled around Lobster Cove's cemetery, cloaking Juelle in a heavy, damp blanket. A sigh escaped her trembling lips. She wasn't supposed to bury her husband after only two years of marriage. She bowed her head, her daughter Makenzie tucked close against her aching chest, asleep, and oblivious to her surroundings. Eugenia sat in the chair to her right, sobbing like a banshee. Irish mourners everywhere would be proud of her grieving mother-in-law. Dressed in black from her Jackie Kennedy style netted hat, to her fashionable black Jimmy Shoo shoes, the woman was in total mourning. She didn't own a black dress, but to appease her mother-in-law's sensibilities, she had worn a black pant suit, and black low-heeled shoes. She drew the line when it came to dressing Makenzie in mourning. She refused to dress a one year old child in black.

Juelle's own heart was numb, her concern at the moment was more for Eugenia than herself. After all, Eugenia had not only lost her husband months ago to a heart attack, but was in the process of burying Sebastian. Her only child. Her world.

She shifted her daughter to her other shoulder, moving her away from the keening Eugenia. The scent of damp, open earth mixed with floral fragrance of the many flower arrangements overpowered her senses.

Between the howling going on beside her, and the heaviness of the air swirling around her, Juelle's head pounded.

She'd met Sebastian at university, fell in love with his easy charismatic charms, and married right after graduation. Her dreams of starting a career, having her own home, and working together with Sebastian to build a new life fell apart when he'd insisted they live with his parents. After all, the McClintock Estate was plenty big enough for two families. Eugenia was ecstatic, and had taken over, expecting her to join the chamber of commerce, the garden club, the church's Ladies of the Rosary Society, and the Lobster Cove Historical Society. Sebastian sided with his mother, telling her it was a great way to meet the 'right' people of Lobster Cove. Not wanting to make waves, she caved. And she hadn't been sorry. Lobster Cove turned out to be one of the most caring communities around.

But now Sebastian was gone—the boating accident had left him paralyzed, in a coma, and on life support. He had hung on for two very long stressful weeks. She'd spent those two agonizing weeks sitting by his bedside—and having to deal with Eugenia's angst. And her best friend, Katelyn—what would she have done without her? She was her rock, her sounding board, and always willing to babysit Makenzie at a moment's notice. Thankfully, Makenzie was a godsend, and a happy baby.

Father Zack, an older priest with gray hair, a full gray beard, and slightly overweight, had served in the Dominican Republic, was well liked in the Lobster Cove community, especially by the teenagers. He stood in front of those assembled and gave the final eulogy.

Eugenia's wailing crescendo became a low moan as those gathered echoed Father Zack's Amen. Eugenia's eyes locked on the casket hovering over Sebastian's final resting place alongside her husband's, hanky in hand. Juelle mumbled Amen along with the others, looked up, and scanned the mass of mourners, well-wishers, Sebastian's schoolmates, fishermen, and friends, as well as a few who showed up at a McClintock funeral just to remain in the wealthy McClintock's good graces. All heads were bowed, except one. Her gaze settled on the tall man in the far back, standing apart from the group. The man exuded a confident, regal presence—and was the spitting image of his father. There was no disputing Hunt McClintock was Hunter McClintock's father, and Sebastian his half-brother—a fact Eugenia tried her level best to dispute.

Hunter acknowledged her with a brief nod, and then disappeared in the crowd. He'd caused such a stir in town already, everyone was abuzz with the news that Hunt McClintock had had a love child before he married Eugenia. How do such rumors get started, anyway?

The crowd broke up. Eugenia leaned over, clutched a handful of fresh soil, hugged it against her chest, then released it and with the help of Günter Jordan, walked out of the cemetery. Several acquaintances stopped by to offer their condolences. A loud burst of uncontrollable sobbing, almost as pathetic as Eugenia's, drew Juelle's, and everyone else's, attention to the left of the mourners. Nora Spears, tall, willowy, blonde, blue eyes, was surrounded by a group of young ladies all trying to console her. Bent over, the woman's beautiful, blemish-free skin was streaked with black mascara and eyeliner from her hysterical sobbing. Juelle didn't know Nora Spears, but had seen her around town with the others—she ran with a different crowd.

Nora broke free and flew at her, arms waving like a madwoman—her long, ruby-red polished nails like talons ready to strike. Juelle stepped aside. What was wrong with this woman? Was she in pain? Did she need someone to call 911?

"You killed him," she shrilled. "You bitch! You killed my Sebastian. You didn't deserve him. You deserve to die for what you did to him."

A bomb had exploded inside Juelle's brain. She couldn't breathe. What the hell was Nora talking about?

Two of Nora's friends surrounded the sobbing woman, tugged on her arms in an effort to hold her back.

"He was going to divorce you and marry me. If you hadn't pulled the plug on him, he'd be mine. All mine."

From out of the blue, Katelyn was by her side. "Let me take Makenzie. Let's get out of here. You don't need to stand here and listen to this."

"You think he worked late every night? Taking care of business?" Nora screeched. "Don't kid yourself. He was with me. He told me everything. Everything!"

"Get your facts straight, Nora. Juelle did not kill Sebastian. He suffered a stroke before anyone had to make that decision."

Juelle found her tongue. "It doesn't matter, Katelyn. It's over. Nora's reaction explains so much. I might have been blindsided by her outburst, but thanks to her, I no longer have to feel guilty about why our marriage fell apart. Why it wasn't working. It wasn't me after all. Let's go before Makenzie wakes up to this sordid scene."

Katelyn took Makenzie and headed to the parking area. Juelle squared her shoulders, raised her head and faced Sebastian's mistress—the person responsible for ruining her marriage. Although to be honest, Sebastian was as much to blame.

"For the record—Katelyn is right. I did not request the hospital to remove Sebastian's life support. From your reaction, I no longer have to carry the responsibility of my broken marriage. I'm sorry for your loss."

Nora fell to the ground on bended knees, gulping for air between sobs, her friends by her side. Stripped of any heartfelt emotions for her cheating husband and his mistress, she followed her friend out of the cemetery.

"I'm so proud of you, girlfriend. I guess you told her."

Katelyn tucked the sleeping Makenzie over her shoulder and rubbed her back. Together, they walked side by side and wound their way along the rutted walkway to the edge of the small cemetery.

Up ahead, on the other side of the church's parking lot, Eugenia was being ushered into the church for the luncheon the St. Joseph's Ladies of the Rosary Society was putting on. With any luck, her mother-in-law had missed the entire scene with Nora Spears. Was her mother-in-law aware of Sebastian's affair?

Nora's outburst left her even more drained than she'd been over the past several weeks. How was she supposed to cope with this new turn of events? Nora's public outburst? Their affair which had taken place right under her nose? And now everyone else knew.

How long had it been going on? She must be in shock because she didn't feel a thing—nothing. Tired, maybe, but not as broken-hearted as she should be about Sebastian's death—or the affair. Although she was saddened at the loss of life. Her daughter would never know her father. Was that how Hunter felt, not having known his father all these years?

Where to turn, who to turn to? Zapped of emotion, she wanted to go home. But where was home? She didn't know. Her parents' home was rented while they were in some godforsaken dot on a map in Africa. And living at the McClintock Estate was uncomfortable at the best of times—it was Eugenia's home, not hers. Eugenia telling her to leave had almost been a blessing, but now that she had no one and nowhere to go, she wasn't so sure.

"I'm so sorry you had to deal with Nora." Katelyn broke her contemplations. "I didn't know. Honest. There had been rumors, of course, but no concrete evidence to substantiate the rumors. If I'd known, I would have told you—you know that, don't you? No matter how hard it would have been for me to tell you, even if it meant our friendship—I would have told you. Honest."

Juelle tugged on her friend's arm. "Katelyn. Stop. I believe you. I trust you. None of this is your fault. I should have known. Suspected something. Unfortunately, I trusted Sebastian and look where faith in our marriage got me. People around here must take me for a fool. How many others were aware of their relationship?" A deep sob escaped. She held her breath, trying to hold her emotions in check, then said the hell with it and let go. "I just don't know where to go from here. What to do. Right now, I want to get away from all these people, all their prying eyes. Their pity. I need time to think and decide what I'm going to do."

"Can I help?" Hunter's words had Juelle and Katelyn swinging around in surprise. His handsome face was pinched, his lips in a straight line, his dark eyebrows shadowed narrowed eyes. How long had he been standing there listening? Had he heard everything? Nora's outburst?

"I couldn't help but overhear the commotion."

That answered her question. She wanted to crawl under a rock and disappear. Could her dismal life get any worse?

"Do you have a magic wand to transport Juelle out of here?" Katelyn asked.

"No, but I can offer my best traveler's escort service and whisk her out of here in my rental chariot. I could use someone to show me the Island while I'm here—check out Cadillac Mountain…"

"Perfect. It will help her unwind, clear her mind. She needs the break."

"Really? People? I'm right here. I think I can talk for myself."

"It's about time. So, I'll take Makenzie home with me and the two of you can make a quick escape before anyone's the wiser."

"But…"

"Go. I've got this covered. Besides, after Nora's outburst, I doubt if any of Eugenia's friends would be surprised if you failed to show up at the luncheon. I know there is no way I'd show up." Katelyn hefted Makenzie up in her arms, turned, and left without another word.

"Wait," Juelle called. Her friend stopped, but didn't turn around. "Let me get the car seat for you. And you might want the diaper bag."

Hunter helped her carry the necessary items to Katelyn's vehicle. Her friend placed Makenzie in the car seat and closed the door.

"Take all the time you need." Katelyn pulled Juelle in for a big teddy bear hug, then released her, and jumped in to her car.

"Come on, my car is over here." Hunter wrapped his arm around her quivering shoulders. It made her want to burrow into him and cry. But she was done crying. He opened the car door for her, and once she was settled, he dashed around the front and slid into his seat. He turned the key in the ignition.

"Sit back and relax. You don't have to say a word. Pretend I'm not here."

Hard to do. His arms around her shoulders had sent warm sizzles racing straight to her core.

"I'm not sure what to say."

"Nothing. Nothing at all. But I'm here in case you do want to talk—get it out of your system. Sometimes talking is the best way to deal with the issue, as my mother would say."

"Does it work for you?"

"Depends on the situation—for the most part, yes."

She tilted her head on the backrest and shut her eyes.

"Put the seat back. Relax. It will help."

"Thanks for rescuing me."

"No problem. We'll take the long route on our way up to Cadillac Mountain. I was there the other day, but the weather was a bit cloudy and I didn't get to see the entire view."

"That sounds wonderful. It's a restful place to visit."

Hunter drove along Route Three, until he came to the visitor center and the Park Loop Road circling around the eastern portion of the island. He turned right onto the one way byway through the forested area and followed the signs past Bear Brook, Beaver Dam Pond, and on up to the Overlook. He pulled into the circular drive, parked, and left the engine running while he sat inside the car staring out at the view. He shut the motor off and sat for fifteen minutes, not wanting to disturb Juelle. She deserved a break after the ordeal at the cemetery. How humiliating was it to learn of your husband's infidelity at his funeral, by his mistress. His heart ached for her—what she must be feeling inside and will carry with her the rest of her life.

Hunter hated his half-brother even more at this moment. If that was the kind of son his father raised, then he was glad his father had left him behind in Hawaii to be raised by his mother.

"Where are we?" Juelle yawned, and sat up in her seat.

"At Lookout Point. I didn't want to wake you, you needed the rest. I was checking out the scenery."

"Thanks. I must have been more exhausted than I thought to pass out so quickly." She brushed her hair back from her face. "Let's get out and walk around so you can get a better view. It really is a lovely spot—you can see way out into the bay."

She stretched when she got out of the car and walked over to the edge. Her beauty and constant caring for others captivated him. He shook uncalled for thoughts out of his head as he watched her body's movements, and then followed her toward the ledge.

Two other couples lingered nearby. A family with three children walked to the far end. He joined Juelle next to the ledge overlooking the ocean, keeping his distance. He didn't think he could control the desire to hold her in his arms—a desire so strong it had been driving him crazy since they'd met at the park the other day—when he'd kissed her out of the blue. It might have been on the forehead, but it had done a number on him. He'd wanted to take her in his arms again. And again, he told himself she was grieving for her husband. Hitting on his half-brother's widow was not cool.

The late afternoon sun was still high overhead, the air warm, and the breeze temperate and cooling. A cruise ship had sailed into Frenchman Bay where it would dock closer to Bar Harbor. White sails dotted the ocean, and below, waves washed up against a craggy, rocky shoreline.

"I never tire of the view. But it's much better from the top of the mountain."

"We're heading there. I took the long way around so you could relax, unwind."

"Have you stopped at Thunder Hole? The trapped air makes a thundering noise when the waves wash through the rock chamber and forces the air out—it's just down the road a bit."

"I stopped the other day. It was packed with tourists enjoying the thunder and the spray. The kids were having a ball climbing down on the boulders and getting soaked. Do you want to stop and check it out?"

"I think I'll pass this time." She laughed. "I don't have the urge to get sprayed."

He liked the way she laughed—it made her eyes sparkle, her whole face light up. He suspected she hadn't had much to laugh about for some time. He might not have known his half-brother, but he sure as hell didn't like him very much right now. It was a fair bet the man took after his mother. How could he cheat on the mother of his child? A beautiful, caring woman at that. The man was a total ass. If he wasn't already dead…

Hunter drove past the jutting rock and Thunder Hole, the spray spritzing across the road drenching everything in its wake. Hunter put his windshield wipers on as they drove through, both laughing at having forgotten to roll up their windows, a bit of spray blowing inside the car.

The road wound around the coast of Otter Point, Little Hunter's Beach, and then wound back into the wooded trail of birch, aspen, oak, and spruce scattered up around Jordan Pond. The traffic pattern changed to accommodate vehicles going in either direction. In silence they continued onto a straight drive past more forested land until Hunter turned the car onto Cadillac Mountain Road. The passage wound upward for a spell before they arrived at the parking lot on the left. He pulled in and turned the ignition off. But before he could come around and open the passenger door for her, Juelle stepped out. He took her hand in his and led her out onto the bare granite rock face sprinkled with three-toothed cinquefoil clusters, the bright sunshine up above, and a sparkling ocean down below.

"I missed the view of Bar Harbor and Lobster Cove the other day. Let's check it out before we go any further."

They stood for a moment, hand in hand, looking down on the Maine coastline. His mind was focused on the softness of her hand, the slender fingers, and short, but neat and unpolished nails. She wrapped those tempting fingers through his, as if their hands knew each other. He forced himself to concentrate on the scenery.

A different view than that from Lookout Point, Bar Harbor lay sprawled out along the coast. To the left, farther up the bay, was the small community of Lobster Cove. McClintock and McClintock Lobster Company building was visible—a large white structure stretching along the inlet, trawlers coming in for the afternoon. Hunter wondered what was to become of the business now that Sebastian was dead. Would Eugenia inherit? Would Juelle?

He tugged on Juelle's hand before his mind could wander any further. Hell, her mind must be going a hundred miles an hour right about now after everything she'd been through. The scene he'd witnessed with the other woman and to find out her husband was a cheat had to be devastating. "Let's check out the rest of the sights while we have such a clear view." He was pleased when she didn't resist.

"You'll love it over on the other side—you can see more of the island." Her voice lacked enthusiasm. He cursed Sebastian again. "Watch your step, there is no path here."

They walked in silence until they reached the other side of the giant boulder. The view was spectacular.

"Jordan Pond is to the left." Juelle pointed out. "We passed it on the Park Loop Road. They have a great little restaurant that serves homemade popovers and fresh squeezed lemonade. There is a stable further on where you can take a carriage ride around this portion of the island, as well. And there are plenty of hiking trails if you like to hike."

"We'll have to go hiking another day."

"I wasn't hinting."

She looked contrite, her eyes wide, those very enticing lips pinched between her teeth. He wanted to kiss them and take her worries away.

"Besides," she continued, "I have Makenzie. I haven't looked into a full-time babysitter or day care—someone besides Katelyn."

"Not a problem. She's a well behaved kid. She can come along for the ride as well."

"We'll see."

"I spied a gift shop when we entered. It's over by the car park. Let's go see if they have a cold soft drink. We can sit down over there, relax, and enjoy more of the view."

Hunter paid for their soft drinks and indicated a spot past the parking lot that overlooked Frenchman Bay.

"Sorry, I don't have a blanket in the car to sit on, but the rock looks clean and dry."

"Glad I wore slacks. I'm not worried about getting them soiled. Although I'm sure Eugenia will have something to say about my attire not being appropriate for attending a funeral. She's very old-fashioned in many respects."

"It must be quite a trial living with her."

"Most of the time it is. But I understand how alone she feels—she has no other family. From what I've been told, she was passed around from one foster home to another from an early age."

"That's no reason to take her frustrations out on you. You're her daughter-in-law, the mother of her granddaughter. You live with her."

"Not for much longer. I plan to find a place of my own soon. I've kept my eye out for a house since Sebastian and I were married, but he always found some excuse not to leave the McClintock Estate. Now I know why. As soon as I find a house within my price range, I won't have to put up with Eugenia."

"Let me know if you need any help looking at houses while I'm here. It will give me something to do besides sitting in my empty motel room waiting for the reading of Hunt's will."

"Eugenia said Mr. Jordan has the meeting set up for Thursday. I'll be glad when this is over and things settle down. Depending on the outcome of the estate, our membership in the Lobster Cove Chamber of Commerce is in question."

Juelle didn't need one more problem added to the already growing list. Her smile turned upside down and her perfect white teeth bit deep into her lower lip. Was that a tear about to escape from the corner of her eye? Oh, crap. Now wasn't the time for his insides to start acting up and sending signals to his brain telling him he needed to hold her, comfort her. He swallowed and shoved his hands in his pockets.

"What's wrong with your membership? Say she no longer controls McClintock and McClintock, can't individuals join as associate members?"

"Yes, but then she wouldn't be a voting member. As it is, the board has been specifically questioning Eugenia's membership. As you've already surmised, she can be difficult to deal with, and they would like nothing better than to find a way to silence her. I'm not worried about my own membership. I only joined at Eugenia's insistence. Eugenia, on the other hand, has been a member forever. In fact, she started the chamber after she and Hunt were married. The board is waiting to learn who is going to inherit the company. It's been in the McClintock family since it started three generations ago. There is a meeting coming up to discuss membership and the Lobster Crawl. I plan to go and make a case on her behalf."

"She looks like the type of person who can stand up for herself."

"Yes, but if she is her usual overbearing self at the meeting, and they can find a loophole to get rid of her voting power, they'll do it. They forget Eugenia has done a lot for the community. Her donations alone have kept many organizations afloat. Without her annual donations to the Lobster Cove Historical Society, the Children's Park Fund, and the McClintock Employees Emergency Fund, families would be finding it hard to stay in Lobster Cove. She was the one responsible for the McClintock Scholarship Fund. And if the company closes, a lot of people will be out of work and needing some of that emergency funding."

"What about your family—your parents? Do they live close by?"

"I'm originally from New York. My parents are missionaries. They're in Africa at the moment. I haven't seen them for several months. Not unusual. I didn't see much of them as a child growing up, seldom see them now. They are committed to their Christian calling. I lived with my grandparents most of the time.

They were very elderly, and died the year I started college."

"That must have been hard on you, not having your parents around."

"Not really. I got used to it. Besides, my grandparents were very caring people—treated me like a daughter. My grandmother took me to all my school events, made sure I got to church, let me have friends over. My grandfather took me fishing—said it was to make sure I was a well-rounded kid."

He wanted to ask her about his father, what kind of a man he was. Besides his looks, did he resemble Hunt McClintock in other ways?

"What about your father? Weren't you ever curious to find out about him?"

Had she read his mind? Hell yes, he had wanted to know about his father. Still did.

Their eyes met. His heart picked up a beat. This beautiful woman was stronger than she gave herself credit.

"I'm sorry. That was insensitive of me." She looked away. "You must be disappointed your father died before you got a chance to meet him. Sebastian, too."

Disappointed was hardly the word he would use, but hell yeah, he wished he had had some form of contact with his father while the man was alive. Sebastian? Not so much.

"My mother was my rock. She never spoke a single unkind word about my father. Even before I made arrangements to fly here, she only had kind words to say. From what she told me, my grandfather was ill and ordered my father back to Maine to take over the business. My mother wrote to Hunt to tell him about her pregnancy, but she received a letter from Herman, my grandfather, that he'd had the marriage annulled. That Hunt had married and his wife was with child. Apparently, the letters crossed in the mail. She wrote to him several times, but never heard back from either of them." He took a breath, shook his head, and continued. "She took what life handed her and lived it day by day, and built a good life for us."

"It couldn't have been easy for her to cope on her own with a child. Did she ever remarry?"

"No, and I never heard her complain. She had a large supporting, loving family." He looked out over the ocean as if to recall his place back in Hawaii. "I know what my mother has told me about the younger man my father was, but what about the older version? What can you tell me about him?"

"Hunt was a very dedicated man—to the company and his employees. He had their best interest at heart. He didn't spend as much time at home, the lobster business required a lot of hours and hard work. Hunt was a kind man, never raised his voice around Makenzie, and always found time to acknowledge her when she was in the room. He was an exceptional man—loyal, good business ethics, and a good family man. You're like him in several respects. Not only do you resemble him, but your mannerisms are like his, and you're a caring person."

"That's kind of you to say."

"Why else would you come to the aid of a damsel in distress?"

She smiled. Her eyes sparkled as she looked into his. Although he had no business doing it, he leaned in and kissed her full on the lips. When she didn't pull back, it was the spark he needed—he pressed his advantage, wrapped his arms around her, and drew her in for a mind-blowing assault to his senses. Her arms curled up around his neck. The kiss continued until he was out of breath, and his lower extremities tightened so hard he was about to embarrass himself. Just in time, she flattened her hands against his chest and leaned back in his arms.

The look in her startled eyes turned a boat-load of screws in his chest. He wasn't going to apologize. That had been one hell of a kiss.

"I'm sorry." She covered her lips with shaking fingers. It was all he could do not to retrieve those fingers and nibble every last one of them. The Maine air must be playing tricks on his libido again, because he'd never been this turned on by a woman's kiss in his entire life.

"You're sorry? I'm the one who should apologize. Although, it's hard not to want to kiss you again."

"Hunter, please. Don't. I should never have let this happen. It's wrong. I was wrong. I just buried Sebastian. What must you think of me?"

Damn. The tears broke his heart. He'd done this to her. He wanted to pull her into his shoulder while she let the tears fall but didn't want to come on too strong. When her tears subsided, he lifted her chin with his fingers and was once again lost by her piercing bold sea-green, but sad eyes. And her very enticing, kissable lips. He wanted to wipe all her worries and sadness away all over again. Lost in a haze of sexual desire, Hunter was shaken from his fantasy when she pulled out of his embrace.

"I think you'd better take me home."

She covered her hot cheeks with shaky hands, and turned her back on him. His insides twisted knowing he had crossed the line and put her in an awkward position.

"Don't beat yourself up. Your husband has been cheating on you. He's gone. You have nothing to feel guilty about. It was only a kiss."

Only a kiss? If he knew how his kisses had made her tingle and her toes curl, making her body ache with desire. Was her shame written all over her face?

"Come on. I'll take you home."

He didn't take her hand this time. Instead, they walked apart, careful not to touch. The ride down Cadillac Mountain was a quiet, nerve-wracking one. Regardless of what he had said, she was bursting with guilt. His voice when he asked for directions to the McClintock Estate startled her, invading her numb brain filled with nothing but Hunter's kiss.

"Sorry. It's on the opposite side of the cove from where you're staying. You passed it on your way to Mariners' Fish Fry on Hidden Cove Drive." And then her mind cleared and she remembered where she'd left her car. "You can drop me off at the cemetery in St. Joseph's parking lot so I can get my car and go pick up Makenzie."

Katelyn would have questions, want details. And she wasn't anxious to answer them.

The church and cemetery parking lot were empty when Hunter pulled his car up next to hers. He put the car in park—she jumped out.

"Thanks," she mumbled, then shut the door.

Hunter had the windows down before she could

take a single step. "I'll pick you up at ten tomorrow. I promised you a day of house hunting."

"Not necessary, thanks."

"Not a problem. A promise is a promise. I'll see you then."

Hunter backed up, pulled out onto the main drive, and looked back at her from his rear-view mirror. He was such a thoughtless ass. He had no business kissing her, let alone on the same day she buried her husband. Sebastian might have been a cheating bastard, but she didn't need anything more to add to her humiliation. He had wanted to kiss her cares away but they had turned into something more, if her reaction was any indication, she was right there with him. And oh boy, what it had done to his insides was much more than he expected. And damn it, he liked it.

Coming to Lobster Cove might have been a bigger mistake than he'd anticipated. Two more days until the reading of his father's will, and he would get out of everyone's life and go back home where he belonged.

In the meantime, he planned to make it up to Juelle and take her house hunting tomorrow, as promised. He'd be a perfect gentleman—no matter how hard it was going to be—and it was going to be one of the most difficult things he'd ever done—he wouldn't touch her.

He swung his car around the cove and headed to Mariner's for one of their lobster rolls and a piece of Mrs. Sullivan's excellent prize-winning blueberry pies.

Chapter Seven

By the time Hunter drove out of the parking lot, she had unlocked her car and gotten into the front seat. She rested her head in her hands on top of the steering wheel. How could she be so attracted to Hunter McClintock? Her husband's half-brother? And so soon after meeting him and burying her husband. She searched for the guilt she had been consumed with on top of the mountain, but it was nowhere to be found. What did that say about her?

She looked at her wedding rings, twisted them between shaking fingers, and bit her lip. Just how long should she continue to wear them without appearing cold and callous? What was the rule in such a situation? Was there a waiting period? She left them on, not wanting to incite her mother-in-law's anger.

And to keep her own emotions in check.

Juelle got out of the car and walked across the lawn to St. Joseph's church. She sent up a prayer of thanks that everyone who had stayed for the luncheon had left. Opening the large oak doors, she slipped inside, dipped her fingers in the white ivory bowl of holy water, made the sign of the cross, and sat in the first pew on the right. With a deep sigh, she sank down on bended knees, bowed her head, and prayed. She prayed for Sebastian's salvation, for peace of mind for Eugenia, and for the strength she would need to carry on alone—

with her fatherless child. Like Hunter's mother, Lani. She sat a moment longer, soaking up the spiritual peace and quiet, letting it surround her like a cloak. Finding a peace within, confident she could face Eugenia later, she quietly walked out of the church to go pick up Makenzie.

Juelle wasn't surprised when she knocked on the front door and Katelyn's fiancée, Sven Olson, opened the door. Sven was tall, with a full head of sand-white hair and blue eyes. Scandinavian by birth, his parents, Inge and Jance, owned the Flower in Bloom flower shop on the corner of Maple and Main Street, where he worked.

"I heard about the riff with Nora Spears at the funeral. Not cool. You doing okay?" He leaned in and gave her a peck on the cheek.

"Already the word has spread. And already it's old news. Believe it or not, I sort of feel sorry for her."

"That's my Juelle—kind heart prevails no matter how bad you're hurting."

"Come on in," Katelyn called behind Sven's back when she joined them in the foyer. "Don't mind him, he doesn't have a sensitive bone in his body at times."

"Do too."

"If you did, you wouldn't have mentioned Nora in the first place."

Katelyn pulled Juelle into a hug. "How'd it go with Hunter? Are you feeling better?"

Juelle gave Sven a pointed stare. It was apparent he understood her silent meaning.

"I was about to leave anyway. The two of you can have all the privacy you need. I have errands to run for the parents." He planted a quick kiss on Katelyn's lips, and then headed for the door. "I'll be back in a couple of hours. Bye."

"Where's Makenzie?"

"Highchair in the kitchen—occupied with a couple of animal crackers. How about a glass of wine?"

Her daughter clapped her hands and extended her hands out to Juelle as she entered the small, but efficient kitchen. "Ma-ma." Juelle picked her up, hugged her, wiped the cookie crumbs off both of their lips, and then placed Makenzie on her lap as she sat down next to the table. Katelyn poured a good portion of white zinfandel into two wine glasses, handed her one, and then placed a platter of cheese and crackers in the center of the oak table, as if she'd been anticipating a friendly chat. Her friend was patient enough to wait until she took a sip of wine before giving her the third degree.

"I've been waiting for the last two hours to find out how you made out with Hunter McClintock. Oops. Wrong wording." Her friend chuckled. "Okay, so what's he like? Other than handsome as sin, I mean? Is he Hunt's son?"

"Whoa. Slow down. He's very caring and kind."

"I saw the way he looked at you. I'd say it's more like smitten."

"Smitten? Give me a break. Now you sound like Eugenia. We've just met. The man feels sorry for me. I just lost my husband only to learn of his infidelity. I was upset. He comforted me."

"Upset? Are you kidding me? The woman ruined your marriage, and you didn't find out until his funeral? How can you be so calm? I've got to tell you, if he wasn't already dead…"

"Well, he is. And to be honest, Katelyn, I don't know how to feel about it, other than to say that a sense of relief and freedom washed over me—freedom from guilt. In fact, Nora must really be in love with him to have reacted the way she did. What does that say about me? I haven't broken down like she did, as if my heart was being ripped wide out and pulled out of my chest. I'm devastated, of course, but there is a part of me that is relieved. How uncaring of me."

"You've had time to adjust. Months of wondering what went wrong, and then to sit by his bedside day after day, worrying, wondering what went wrong—if he was going to live. You were prepared for the worse. And living through a rocky marriage since Makenzie was born, your heart wasn't deeply involved any longer. You've been falling out of love with Sebastian the last few months. You have nothing to feel guilty about."

"That's the sad part. I grieve for Sebastian, and Eugenia's loss, but guilty…? It's turning on and off inside of me like a water faucet. I don't know how to feel."

"I'd be careful where Hunter McClintock is concerned if I were you. Make sure he's the real deal before you get involved. Sven is right—you're too kind-hearted. With all you've been through at the hands of the McClintocks, you're still compassionate where they are concerned. They don't deserve to have you in the family. Especially, Eugenia."

"I won't have to deal with her on a daily basis much longer. She asked me to leave. Can you believe it? After all this time of wanting to walk out, she finally admits she doesn't want me there?"

"Asked you? Or told you?"

"It doesn't matter. Hunter is taking me house hunting tomorrow."

"Hunter? Whoa. Back to my original question. What transpired on that ride up to Cadillac Mountain and are you sure you know what you're doing?"

Juelle's face flamed. She lowered her head, took another sip of wine, and munched a cracker.

"Juelle? Just how comforting was Hunter?"

"He's a kind man," she mumbled with her mouth full.

"Kind, my foot. I don't care if you buried Sebastian today. He was a lying, cheating jerk, and you deserve so much better. Kindness from another man is nothing to be embarrassed about, but make sure you know what you're up against. Take your time. Don't rush things."

"I keep telling myself that. But you don't understand…"

"He kissed you, didn't he?"

Her throat closed up, her face so hot just thinking about Hunter's sensual, erotic kisses, she was sure an ice cube would melt in seconds if it came in contact with her body.

"Aha! He did. Good for you. He's one hunk of a man. And his body is very fit looking, if you ask me. Wonder what he does for a living? You said he lives in Hawaii? With his tan, I bet he's a surfer."

"He is. But he and his mother own a travel company."

"Ahhh, Hawaii. Always dreamed of going there for a vacation someday. Sven not so much, he loves the fishing life here—must be the Scandinavian in him. I've got to admit, I love living here in Lobster Cove, too."

"It does grow on you, doesn't it? I feel as if this town has always been my home. I hope I can find a place to live close by. And raise Makenzie here. It's a great community and I've made so many wonderful friends."

"After living at the McClintock Estate, it's going to be hard to climb down a notch."

"Nope. It's always been too much for me—I don't fit in there. I want something small, cozy, like this place. A nice yard for Makenzie."

"I noticed there are a few places holding open houses this week. Let me grab the Lobster Cove Anchor newspaper and we can see what's available."

Juelle hugged her daughter, tickled her tummy, and the two of them laughed. Makenzie wrapped her tiny arms around Juelle's neck and the two of them snuggled.

"Soon, sweetie. We will have our own home, soon."

"Here it is. Let's see what's available."

Juelle placed Makenzie back in the highchair, gave her another cookie, a cup of milk with a sippy lid, and then joined her friend as they put their heads together over the newspaper, happier than she'd been in a long time. Was this going to happen? She sighed. A house? A home of her own? At last?

"Look here. Jessica Martin Real Estate Agency has several homes listed as having open houses this week."

"I know Jessica. She's a member of the Chamber of Commerce. I'll give her a call and see if she's available tomorrow."

They scanned through the various entries, jotting

down several locations.

"There's two on Birch Avenue at the end of town, and one on Aspen Avenue, close to the school and Grant's Lake. That might be a good location."

"Here's one on Second Street. More residential. Still, it's not a bad location—off the main drag. Worth checking out. Oh, Katelyn, I can't believe I'm doing this. It's rather exciting."

"Have you considered how you're going to afford a home of your own? I know the McClintock's have money, but what about you?"

"I have to check with the bank to see what funds are available. I've been able to set some aside, and I applied for a teaching position at the school for this fall."

"What? You didn't mention that—when did you put in your application?"

"A few months ago when I considered filing for a divorce. I knew I'd need to find a job at some point."

"You're more on top of things than I thought." Katelyn gave her a lopsided smile and tapped the newspaper with her fingers. "If you need me to go back with you for a second look at any of these homes, let me know. I'd offer to babysit tomorrow, but Sven and I have plans."

"Not to worry. I'm taking Makenzie with me. After all, it's going to be her home too. If she gets antsy inside any of them, then it isn't the house for us."

"Really? Bad vibes from the kid?"

"Laugh, but the house has to fit both of us."

****

Later that night, after she and Katelyn identified three places to check out the next day, Juelle prepared

Makenzie for bed. After a warm tub bath with her daughter's favorite yellow ducks, red plastic lobster squeaky bath toy, and her princess washcloth, Juelle found herself just as wet as her daughter. And both laughing, snuggling and happy.

"Come on, Sweet Pea, let's get you dried, powdered, and ready for bed."

She loved this time of night with her daughter. Rocking her to sleep each night always made her heart burst with love. She hummed softly while Makenzie finished her bottle and closed her eyes. After settling her in the crib and making sure the baby monitor was on, she placed a soft kiss on her forehead.

It was time to face Eugenia.

She found her mother-in-law sitting in her favorite chair facing the glassed-in patio overlooking the harbor and Frenchman Bay beyond. The tide had drifted out for the evening, leaving behind narrow channels, and tufts of American beach grasses sticking out of the sand and mud along the coast line. Lights from across the harbor sparkled in the clear, star-studded night. The Martin Lighthouse's beam blinked as its high-powered signal rotated. She would miss these sights when she left the estate. She had spent many hours in this room, holding Makenzie when she first came home from the hospital, then on summer evenings where they would relax together while Eugenia attended various meetings without her, and Sebastian was supposedly at work. And the sun shining through the floor-to-ceiling picture window early in the mornings always brightened her day. The houses she'd identified to look at tomorrow weren't close to the shoreline, but whatever she decided on, it would be hers. She could live with that and without this view.

A hand-woven Egyptian rug sprawled between the two wing-backed chairs, a low glass-topped coffee table separating them. Juelle's slippered footsteps padded across the polished hardwood floor. She sat across from Eugenia and looked out the window. Eugenia ignored her presence. Silence ensued for several minutes before Juelle broke the spell.

"I'm sorry about today, Eugenia. I had no idea Nora Spears and Sebastian were involved in an affair. Her outburst was a complete shock."

"Nor did I. I'm also sorry you had to be inflicted with such abhorrent actions by that trollop."

Juelle almost laughed at the antiquated term. She cleared her throat instead and let Eugenia continue.

"How utterly embarrassing. However, that doesn't account for you not attending the luncheon the Ladies of the Rosary Society put on for us. I was left to face everyone by myself. Father Zack was looking for you and wanted to offer his condolences. I had to lie to a priest, for God's sake, and tell him you were so distraught, you returned home to grieve in private."

"Thank you. I'm sure you handled it well. And I'm sure you've been aware that things have been strained between me and Sebastian. I want you to know I tried my best to make things right between us, but nothing I did seemed to work. Now I understand why nothing I could say or do made any difference with Sebastian. Please know I never wished Sebastian any harm. I would never have asked the doctor's to remove life support without your consent."

Eugenia remained quiet as she gazed out the window. Juelle closed her eyes, sighed, and sat back in the cushioned chair. An uncomfortable silence echoed off the walls. Eugenia's whispered words broke the silence.

"I never wanted him to go out to sea—to become a fisherman. He had such great potential. With his business major, I assumed he would join the company in the office, become the manager. But the adventure of the open sea called to him. He wanted to be like Hunt, experience the thrill of the outdoors—not be shut up indoors, day after day."

"Then he died doing what he loved to do. We have to keep that in mind, and not look at the 'what might have beens'."

"You are being too kind after what he's done to you. You are much more preferable than that…that…jezebel."

If Eugenia's back-handed compliment hadn't ended with another one of her comical, antiquated terms, Juelle would have been hurt. As it was, in Eugenia's eyes, no one would ever have been good enough for Sebastian. In Eugenia's own way, she was being kind.

"I wanted to let you know I'll be attending several open houses offered through Jessica Martin Realty tomorrow. Katelyn and I identified three places that appeared to be suitable, and I've already contacted Jessica. She's arranged to meet me. I can't promise I'll be moving out as soon as you'd like. These things take time. But I am in the process."

Mumbled huffing came from the other chair. Juelle wondered just what her mother-in-law's problem was now. She didn't have long to wait.

"Are you planning on taking my granddaughter

away from me, as well?"

Shocked at the unexpected concern for her granddaughter—a granddaughter she hadn't spent much time with to date, too busy with all her many clubs and organizations—Juelle took a moment to collect her sanity. Eugenia certainly kept her on her toes. She hadn't had long to wait for her mother-in-law to play the trump card called guilt.

Wanting to roll her head to release the tension in her shoulders, she took a deep breath instead.

"I don't plan to leave Lobster Cove. I'll be close by, and you can have all the access to Makenzie you want. I would never keep your granddaughter from you, Eugenia."

"Thank you."

Eugenia's mild tone caught her off-guard. Was there more to her mother-in-law than she realized? Had she been right to feel sorry for her all this time?

"On another note, I'm hearing rumors you've been hanging around with that man who claims to be my husband's son. You should be careful, he's not who he says he is. There is no proof he's Hunt's son. He can only be here to collect from the family's estate. These scam artists are everywhere these days. I want you to stay away from him. We can't have you tarnishing the McClintock name by being seen with this man."

Tarnishing the family name? Was she kidding? As if Sebastian hadn't already done that? Just when she thought Eugenia had turned amiable, she struck again.

Juelle sat up in her chair and shot Eugenia a warning glance she hoped the woman would understand. It was past time she stood up for herself. Sebastian was dead. She was moving out of the

McClintock Estate. She had a mind of her own, and she wasn't going to let this woman dictate her every move one minute longer.

"Are you telling me who I can, and can't see?"

Eugenia sat forward and returned the glare. Juelle refused to back down and raised her eyebrows.

"Just so you and your friends know, Hunter McClintock is the one taking me house hunting tomorrow."

"*No!*"

Eugenia fell back in her chair and put her hand over her heart. It was just too comical. Juelle had to leave before she laughed in Eugenia's face.

"Yes. And he is Hunt's son. All you have to do is look at the man to see the resemblance. Don't tell me you haven't noticed? Look at the pictures you have of your husband when he was younger—they could almost be twins, the resemblance is uncanny."

"I've got Günter Jordan working on proving that man is a fraud. If you won't heed my warning, you'll only have yourself to blame when his scam is revealed."

"I don't think Mr. Jordan would have been foolish enough to contact a con artist for the reading of Hunt's will. What would be gained by spinning his wheels to locate an imposter?"

Juelle took advantage of Eugenia's stunned silence at her confrontation. Determined their conversation was over, Juelle left her mother-in-law to stew on her own. There was no pleasing the woman. She was done trying to understand her and appease her at every pessimistic turn.

She was going to do nothing but look ahead from

now on. Cinderella had kissed a prince today. It was time to hold her head up—face her demons, and live her life her way.

She put a smile on her face as she made her way up the staircase. She stood tall, squared her shoulders, and dashed the rest of the way up the stairs to the second floor landing and down the hall. The motion was so freeing, once inside her room she swung around and flopped down on the bed, her arms swinging wide. Her last thought before she fell asleep, fully dressed, was whether or not Hunter McClintock would kiss her again.

Chapter Eight

After calling Hunter to tell him she'd meet him at the park at ten, instead of him picking her up at the estate, she left a note for Eugenia saying she'd be gone all day. She dressed in casual lightweight aqua capris, a white silk spaghetti-strap blouse with matching aqua trim, and slipped into a comfortable pair of tan sling-backs. Despite the forecast calling for another hot June day, Juelle grabbed a sweater for Makenzie in case the homes they visited were too cool for the sleeveless pink romper set. She ran a comb through her unruly hair and tucked it behind her ears.

With Makenzie settled in the car seat, and the ever ready bag on the floor, Juelle anticipated the day ahead. Hunter was waiting for them when she pulled in to a parking spot next to the Captain's Library off First Street.

"I hope you don't mind I brought Makenzie with me. Katelyn and Sven had other plans today, and Eugenia isn't the babysitting kind of grandmother, although she swears she wants to start spending time with her granddaughter."

"Not a problem. You lift her out of the car seat and I'll transfer it to my car."

The two worked together shifting Makenzie's necessities, then climbed into Hunter's Kia, ready to get started.

"Where to? I've seen a few For Sale signs as I've driven around town, but I'm not sure which ones you have in mind."

"Katelyn and I checked the papers last night. The Jessica Martin Real Estate Agency has several open houses she's showing today. I gave her a call, and she agreed to meet us and show us around the three I found interesting. The first one is out on Birch Avenue."

"Give me the address and I'll plug it into the GPS."

Once the GPS was set, Hunter backed out onto First Street, and then took a right onto Birch. The first house was three miles out, close to the entrance of Acadia National Park. It was tucked into a wooded area, the last house before the visitor center. Although it was very secluded, Juelle wasn't sure it would work.

Jessica Martin, a young, strikingly beautiful businesswoman in her mid-twenties, met them at the front door with a pleasant smile on her face.

"I've got to admit, I was surprised to hear from you, Juelle. I didn't know you were in the market for a house. I'm tickled you chose me to help you find something." The young realtor extended her hand. Juelle shifted Makenzie on to her left hip, and shook Jessica's hand.

"This is Hunter McClintock. Hunter, Jessica Martin. She's a member of the Lobster Cove Chamber of Commerce."

"Yes, I saw him at the service yesterday." She offered him her hand as well. "Glad to meet you. Are you moving to Lobster Cove?"

"No. I'm only here for a few more days, but offered to help Juelle while I'm here."

"Well, come on in. I think you'll like this place.

It's rather charming, even though it's close to the park entrance. There is a large backyard, already fenced in, but there are no other houses beyond—it's all woodland. It's pretty shaded most of the year, but it has a fantastic fireplace, and the kitchen is to die for. Let me show you."

Jessica was right, the interior layout was something out of a House Beautiful or Architectural Digest. The cathedral ceilings, with a large loft bedroom and private bath was impressive.

Makenzie was fussing by the time they finished going through the rooms on the main floor and headed down to the basement.

"Here, let me take her out back and wander around the yard while you finish inspecting things down here." Hunter reached for Makenzie. "I'll meet you out front when you're finished."

Makenzie went to him without a fuss. Hunter had been patient and helpful with Makenzie, so far, she hated to admit it, but she was glad he'd offered to drive her around to the open houses today, so she could concentrate on the homes.

Jessica smiled as Hunter took Makenzie and headed back up the stairwell. Juelle sensed Jessica's curiosity, but was thankful the realtor didn't pry. Juelle wasn't about to offer an explanation of why Hunter was with her today, or how content Makenzie was to be held by Hunt's son. She didn't have an explanation to give. Being a member of the Chamber of Commerce, Jessica would be one of those considering terminating Eugenia's membership—she didn't want to antagonize Jessica and ruin any chances Eugenia might have of retaining her membership. Thankfully, the realtor was all business, and continued without questioning her.

"As you can see the basement is dry, and there are no signs of leakage anywhere. The previous owner attempted to put a family room down here, but he received a job offer down south, so never finished before he had to relocate. It wouldn't take much to complete and make it fit your own needs."

"To be honest, it's a gorgeous home, but too far out, and too close to the park."

"With your baby, I understand. The house farther down, closer to town might work. It's on a cul-de-sac off the main street, so you wouldn't get the traffic. If you'll follow me in your car, I'll show it to you."

Juelle loved the second house, but held out until they were shown the one at the northern end of town on Aspen Avenue. Which turned out to be perfect.

Juelle followed Jessica up the sidewalk leading to the large wrap-around, screened in front porch. Hunter, carrying Makenzie, followed. Jessica held the screen door open for them, then pulled her keys out and opened the front door. Juelle's mouth dropped as soon as she stepped inside.

"Jessica! This is the one. Oh, my goodness. I love how those windows overlook the harbor. What a magnificent view. Who would have thought that this far back you would have such a wonderful view of Frenchman Bay, too?"

"It's open to the morning sun and the bay on this side of the house. You can't see it from the road, but it sits on a slight incline and is situated so there are no obstructions to the view. As you know, Maine is the first State to get the morning sunrise—you won't have to miss a one. Now, the west side of the house is partially shaded so you'll get some afternoon and evening sun, but it's a comfortable yard with plenty of shade in summer, and blocks some of the winter wind. And, wait until you see the rest of the house, I think you'll love it even more. Oh, and Grant's Lake is only a mile or so away in the other direction. Makes for a nice stroll."

The modern, ranch style home had a two-car garage attached at an angle to the side of the house. The large fireplace in the main room, the efficient, well-appointed kitchen, and back sundeck, stone grill and the wide expanse of a lawn made Juelle want to move in today.

"It's perfect," she sighed. "What do you think, Hunter? Isn't it perfect?"

Hunter, who had been playing with Makenzie during the entire tour, finally spoke.

"It does appear to be in good condition. How old did you say the house is?" He turned to the realtor. "What about the utilities? Taxes? What other expenses are involved?"

Once again, Juelle was glad Hunter was on hand and had followed them around the house. She'd been so taken with the visual aspects of the house and envisioning living there with Makenzie that she forgot about all the important details he mentioned. She'd been so excited about taking that first step to move out of Eugenia's, and having a place and a life of her own, she hadn't considered the important facts, like the finances involved and how she was going to afford the place. Was she really ready to be a homeowner?

"The house is twenty years old. The owner was an architect. As for the other details, if you think this is the house for you, we can go in the dining room where I set up a card table and can spread everything out and discuss them."

An hour later, her mind swimming with details she'd no idea she needed to deal with, and wondering how she was going to finance it all, her mind buzzed with the reality of owning her own home.

"I have to be honest and remind you that this property is one of those on the open house listing. I expect several other interested buyers to stop by today—some of them might decide to make an offer. But, I'll tell you what I can do. Because you're sure you want this house, and I know the McClintock credit is excellent, I'll hold it for you for the next twenty-four hours. Afterward, if anyone else is interested, I'll have to give them the opportunity to make a purchase offer."

"I appreciate your consideration, Jessica. I do love the house, and feel this is the one for me and Makenzie. As soon as I contact the bank to work through the specifics, I'll be in touch."

"Great. I do have another couple looking at the place in about ten minutes. I'll let you see yourselves out. I'll see you at the chamber meeting. Have you any ideas for the Lobster Crawl this year? Who's heading it up?"

"I'm pretty sure Eugenia is leading the committee. But we haven't discussed it. I think the Friends of the Library want to do something. Maybe set something up at the park—a lobster dish cook-off where each business competes and visitors choose the winner. Kind of like those chili cook-offs you read about."

"Sounds like a great idea. Let's mention it at the meeting. See you then."

Juelle, and Hunter, who was holding Makenzie, stepped off the front porch as an older couple strolled up the sidewalk. The couple smiled and nodded to them as they walked past to greet Jessica, who waited for them on the porch.

"What a lovely family," the woman said to the realtor. If Jessica answered, Juelle didn't hear her. Her insides smiled at the comment. Had Hunter heard the woman's comment? She didn't dare look at him to determine whether he had heard the comment, or see his reaction. He was silent as they approached his vehicle. She took Makenzie from his arms and gave her daughter a hug.

"How about lunch?" he asked. "It's such a gorgeous day, we can head out to Jordan Pond House for a bite to eat, and then maybe see about a carriage ride."

"You don't have to cater to us all day, Hunter."

"I'm at loose ends. I could use the company."

"What about Makenzie?"

"Not a problem. She's a well behaved kid, and we seem to be hitting it off together. She'll love it. Say yes."

Juelle wasn't sure spending an entire day with Hunter was a good idea. But then, she remembered Eugenia demanding her not to have anything to do with him. Too bad. She liked him. More than she should so soon after meeting him. But she wasn't ready to go back to the estate and face Eugenia.

"I'd love to. Their lobster stew is to die for, not to mention their popovers. But I'll need to be back before the bank closes this afternoon so I can check on my finances and see about a loan."

Hunter drove them up to Jordan Pond where they found an umbrella covered wooden picnic tables on the lawn overlooking the pond. Views of Penobscot Mountain and the Bubbles rose in the background on the other side of the pond. Juelle placed a blanket on the lawn for Makenzie, while she and Hunter took advantage of their baby-free arms to eat.

"What's this Lobster Crawl you were talking about with the realtor?"

"The Chamber is looking to enhance tourism in Lobster Cove. With the economy on a downswing, they're trying to boost business and bring in some of the tourists who frequent Bar Harbor and Acadia."

"It sounds like fun. Maybe I should consider a luau cook-off back on the islands." He chuckled as if he'd made a joke. Makenzie clapped her hands and giggled along with him. He tweaked her nose, and she laughed all the more.

"What a great idea. But isn't a luau a big deal on the Islands?"

"Not as a cook-off, per se. Our travel company does do similar events on occasion. We cater mostly to tourists who come in on major cruise lines and schedule tours around the islands, although we do have cruise/tours to other islands in the Pacific. On occasion, we have special events for our return patrons. I play tour guide on many of the tours. What about you? What do you do here on this island?"

Juelle looked out over the pond. She was embarrassed to admit she was a stay-at-home mom.

"Other than serving on various organizations' committees that Eugenia belongs to, not much. Sebastian and I married right after college, and then moved to the McClintock Estate. According to Eugenia, a McClintock wife does not work for a living—they serve the community."

"Serving the community is a worthwhile endeavor. And you are raising a child. Nothing wrong with that."

"I didn't mean it to sound as if I didn't enjoy either. Some look at it as indulgent, or a sacrifice. I feel as if I'm wasting my education."

"What was your major? What would you rather be doing?"

A good question. Now that she had Makenzie she wasn't sure she wanted to leave her daughter with anyone else while she worked. But could she afford to buy a house and still be a stay at home mom? She wouldn't have Sebastian's income now, and she had no idea if he had life insurance. She'd have to check with Mr. Jordan to see what her financial status was now that Sebastian was gone.

"Education, with a teaching certificate. After two years of not having to work, I've put in an application at the high school. But like everything else, this is all new to me. Maybe something part-time until Makenzie starts school."

"With a degree in education, I'm sure you'll be able to find something if your application isn't accepted. Seems to me there's a lot of history on this Island."

"Yes, and seeing as I belong to the historical society, I know a bit about the Island's history. Jordon Pond is one of those historic locations that's about to change hands. The Jordan House was opened in 1870, and has been run by the Acadia Corporation. Not sure who the new owners are, but I'm glad it's going to continue. It's a charming place for visitors to enjoy."

"What's the history behind the McClintock and McClintock Lobster Company?"

The question caught her off guard. She was sure the status of the McClintock holdings would come up when she talked to them at the bank, as well, and was prepared.

"Historically, Herman McClintock arrived on the islands as a young lad back in the day. A fisherman by trade, he started a local fishery with a single boat. When the island started to grow, he hired a few young men and bought another boat and sold to local businesses. Before he knew it, his business was shipping all over the east coast. He married Marian Landers. They had one child, a son, Hunt McClintock—your father. When he became old enough to join the company, Herman changed the name of the company to McClintock and McClintock Lobster Company. Before Herman passed, Hunt took over and started looking for international connections. I think that's when he must have gone to Hawaii and met your mother. When Herman died, Hunt became sole owner. You know the rest. Now with both Hunt and Sebastian gone, I don't know what's going to happen to the business."

"Perhaps Eugenia is next in line."

"Or you. You are Hunt's son."

"We'll have to wait until the will is read tomorrow afternoon and see what develops. What about Sebastian's will? Did he have one?"

"If he did, we didn't discuss it. In fact, we hadn't done anything about providing for Makenzie should something happen to either of us. Something I'll have to talk to Mr. Jordan about."

"Good plan. In the meantime, let's finish up here and go catch one of those buggy rides around the island."

"I'm going to have to take a rain check if I want to get to the bank today before it closes."

****

Later that afternoon, Juelle sat across from Loan Officer Tempest Yarbrough, biting her lower lip and wringing her hands in her lap. Being turned down for a loan now, despite being a McClintock, was another setback she didn't need. She'd never before had to apply for a mortgage from a bank. The only finances she'd had to deal with was working her way through college. Her grandparents had saved for her education, which had been a complete surprise. Her parents being missionaries, on the other hand, lived frugally and weren't able to help.

"I don't understand. What do you mean I don't have access to the accounts?"

"I'm sorry, Mrs. McClintock, the only account I can help you with is the joint account with your name on it. Your name is not on any of the other accounts Sebastian set up."

"But I'm his wife! Sebastian is dead. Doesn't that give me the right to them?"

Her own account wasn't substantial enough to garner a loan even if she had wanted to purchase an old fishing hut out in the middle of the ocean.

"Not necessarily. One of the accounts is a joint account with someone else."

"What?" Juelle's head shot up. "Who?"

"I'm not at liberty to say."

Tempest had the grace to look embarrassed and

sympathetic. She didn't want sympathetic. She wanted answers.

"If his mother's name is on the account, I understand. Or did he put Makenzie's name on one?"

That would make sense in a weird sort of way. At least he had taken care of his daughter's future.

"I'm sorry. And I'm sorry about the loan. If you had more collateral, I could approve it today."

"I'm sorry, too. Is there anyone else I can talk to who can give me that information?"

"Honey, I don't think you want to go there. Why not just let it alone." Tempest lowered her eyes, fumbled with the papers in front of her as if she were so engrossed in its contents she forgot she had a client in the room.

What the hell was this woman talking about? Why should she let it alone? What was the big secret? Oh, no! Did Sebastian have a separate account with Nora Spears' name on it? Nora had said Sebastian planned to divorce her and marry Nora. Had he been planning this all along? Been setting money aside just for them?

Juelle's head shot up. She stared, unseeing, into Tempest's compassionate eyes, her own mind buzzing with anger. She shoved her chair back from the table, and stood, her purse up over her shoulders, her fists clenched at her sides. Her insides shook with the implication of what that meant. Sebastian had loved Nora Spears and had planned to leave her for the other woman. Why he hadn't ask for a divorce, she didn't know, would never know, but it would have been better than having Tempest Yarbrough know and have kept his secret. How many others in Lobster Cove were privy to information about his affair? If Nora's cohorts knew, it was a safe bet everyone who had been at the funeral and witnessed Nora's outburst knew, too. Which meant the entire town was also aware.

"I am sorry, Juelle. There is no way I could have told you. It wasn't my place. If there is anything else I can do for you, please let me know."

"I have to let Jessica Martin know I can't afford the house."

Juelle stepped out into the hot afternoon heat. Sweat trickled down her back. She wanted to scream. She hadn't seen that one coming. What other secrets did Sebastian take to the grave with him?

She crossed Second Street and walked across the park where the large white tent was being set in place for the Oil and Water Art Festival that was taking place for the Father's Day weekend. The event was designed to showcase Maine's arts and artists, cohosted by the gallery owners. Lincoln Shattuck was the driving force behind the event. This year, Ginny Brent, a guest judge from New Hampshire was slated to be on hand. The tent would be filled with paintings and sculptures, with other local high-end crafters spread out around town.

Juelle had planned to attend the event, but now her heart wasn't in it. She found her way around the activity to a secluded bench surrounded by two huge rhododendrons closer to Oak Avenue. Their lavish rounded blooms of shaded lavender covered the entire bush, but their beauty did little to warm her heart. Bees buzzed in drunken ecstasy as they sucked at the pollen. Juelle sat, lips pinched, hands clasping the edge of the wooden bench, her mind stuck in neutral, going nowhere. Tears threatened.

What the hell was she going to do now? How was

she ever going to be able to afford to move out of the McClintock Estate?

****

Hunter walked out of Sweet Bea's with an extra-large coffee, and a meat pie he was assured was a favorite of the tourists, as well as the locals. He crossed the street to the park intent on finding a bench where he could sit and try to make some sense of the strong magnetism Juelle McClintock had on his psyche. He had been sucker-punched the first time he laid eyes on her, and his feelings had escalated. And after the time he'd spent with her and Makenzie this morning, he couldn't get her out of his mind.

He downed the meat pie in four bites, followed it down with coffee, and made his way across Oak Avenue. And damned if Juelle wasn't sitting on one of the benches shaded by two maples and surrounded by purple rhododendrons, as if she was trying to hide from the world. He drew closer, her sadness evident in the downcast face, the white knuckles grasping the bench, her stillness. He almost didn't want to disturb her, but the woman had a way of having his heart catch every time he looked at her, let alone being within the same time zone—or thinking of her. He gulped his coffee as he continued across the lawn, and made an effort to calm his beating heart. What the hell had happened between the time they'd had lunch at Jordan Pond and now to put her in such a funk?

"I take it things didn't go well at the bank?" He approached, wanting to lean down and wipe away her tears—his heart ached for her.

She looked up in surprise, brushed her fingers over her cheeks, and then scooted aside, an invitation for him to sit. He didn't hesitate.

"That's putting it mildly," she sniffed. "I wish I'd had the gumption to divorce Sebastian months ago, instead of waiting."

"What'd he do now? Clean out the accounts?" It was almost a joke, but the more he considered it, the more he came to the conclusion that it would be something the cheat would do.

"That would almost be preferable. No, he had a separate account with Nora Spear's name on it. I can't touch it, nor his other accounts until his holdings are cleared. I'm sure Mr. Jordan will handle this, as well. Mr. Jordan happens to be 'the' family lawyer."

"I'm so sorry, Juelle. I didn't mean to make a joke of it. I wasn't thinking." He set the coffee on the bench, and wrapped her in his arms, pulling her into his chest. Her understated perfume, the fresh scent of coconut shampoo, and baby powder had his insides melting, and other parts of him growing hard at the same time. He didn't care if Sebastian was his half-brother, he hated him at this very moment. More than he even hated his father. He almost wished his mother had remarried and changed his last name. He wasn't proud to be a McClintock right now.

He helped her sit back on the bench and wished he could take all her hurt away, take her away from all this. He kissed the top of her head, tilted her head on his shoulder, and kept his arm around her. Damn it, if they weren't in the wide open spaces in the middle of the park with men erecting tents, he'd kiss her like he meant it—like he had up on Cadillac Mountain. The woman had stolen his heart.

He held his breath as she wrapped her arms around

his ribs and snuggled deeper. He let her, even though the grip on his own restraints dwindled—fast. No woman had ever gotten to him like this—he'd guarded his heart for so long, and he had to come all the way to Lobster Cove to have it ripped wide open.

He ran his fingers through her hair, silky soft, the sun shining on it like spun burnish gold. He gathered her closer. She slid next to him, their hips just about overlapping. Any closer and she'd be on his lap, which wouldn't upset him in the least.

"And on top of that," she hiccupped. "I don't have enough collateral to get a loan to cover the cost of the house."

"Have you checked with your mother-in-law? Do you think she would co-sign for a loan?"

"Not in this lifetime." She sat up, pulled a tissue from her purse, and wiped her face. "Sorry. I didn't mean to cry all over your shirt."

"It'll dry. Are you going to be okay?"

"At least I'm not homeless. I doubt Eugenia will kick me and Makenzie out of the house until I can find something. Deep down, I don't think she's that heartless."

Her smile warmed his heart.

"I keep thinking about her background. If she was a foster child and was shifted from home to home, I doubt she'd be up to seeing her own granddaughter homeless."

His heart swelled. Not only did she have the stamina to deal with difficult situations and still find the good in others, she was a survivor. He helped himself to the kiss he hadn't been able to get out of his head all day. To hell with anyone catching them at it. The woman had been cheated on, her husband was deceased, and she needed to know someone found her desirable. And hell, she was way more than just desirable. She was a slice of heaven sent down from above just for him. His heart fluttered. He'd have to be careful or he'd find himself caring for her more than he should.

"Maybe things will ease up after your father-in-law's will is read. Did Sebastian leave a will?"

How the hell was she going to cope on her own if she couldn't even secure a loan for a home?

"No. There is no will that I'm aware of. It doesn't make much difference. Sebastian didn't own anything except his car, and the bank accounts. Tempest Yarbrough at the bank didn't think there was enough to cover a mortgage. But you have a point. I'll make an appointment with Mr. Jordan and contact Jessica Martin, explain the situation, see if she'll give me a little more time."

Chapter Nine

Hunter sat at the far end of the oblong table in the simply appointed conference room in anticipation of Günter Jordan reading his father's will. Eugenia McClintock sat at the opposite end, next to Mr. Jordan, and Juelle found a seat across from them. He didn't want to be here—it was like opening a can of worms that turned out to be full of viperous snakes. Eugenia's confident smile as she faced Juelle across the table was annoying. His heart ached for Juelle, the silent anticipation must be hell for her, having to face these people after the punch in the gut at the bank yesterday. Had she told her mother-in-law about her ass-hole son's further deception? His blood boiled, but he tamped his anger down. This was not the time or place to act out. It would only make it harder on Juelle.

Günter Jordan cleared his throat and addressed the three of them.

"Thank you all for coming and being on time. There are a few preliminaries to get out of the way before we get to the main portion of Hunt's wishes."

"We can dispense with all those boring details Günter—just get on with the important particulars."

Günter met Hunter's eyes across the room. Hunter nodded in agreement. The lawyer turned to Juelle, who also nodded.

"All right then. Hunt McClintock was adamant he

recognize his son Hunter McClintock from a previous marriage to one Lani Aka McClintock, and was unwavering that in order to make amends, she be mentioned in his last requests."

"*NO!*" Eugenia jumped from her chair. "I won't hear of it. It's not true. He is not Hunt's son! This woman has not been in his life all these years! I have."

"Sit down, Eugenia," Günter raised his voice, his face pinched, as if he was disappointed in her outburst. "I'm not finished."

Eugenia sat, her hands going to the region where her heart was supposed to be, her face turning a pasty shade of white. The woman had a point, however, it was his mother she'd referred to and he took exception to this heartless woman's outburst. He kept quiet, and waited to see what else Mr. Jordan had to say.

"Now then. Where was I?" The lawyer shuffled the papers in front of him. "Here it is. Lani Aka McClintock is to receive a lump sum in the amount of $500,000."

Eugenia gasped. Hunter shook his head. His mother would be surprised at the amount of her inheritance. He glanced over at Juelle. She was observing her mother-in-law with concern—her own face pale, drawn. Dammit it. Hadn't Juelle suffered enough? How could he make this right for her?

"I have here two letters. One for Hunter, and one for Hunt's first wife Lani."

He handed two separately sealed envelopes to Hunter. Hunter took them and tucked them in his shirt pocket.

"Now. To Eugenia, my second wife," Jordan continued. "I leave the McClintock Estate, which includes its contents, grounds, and a two million dollar trust sufficient to maintain the estate and support her for the rest of her life."

Eugenia sat silent. Her eyes glued to the lawyer.

When no one commented, Günter Jordan pressed on. "As for the business of McClintock and McClintock Lobster Company, located at Pier One, Lobster Cove, Maine, and all the assets connected with the business, they are to be controlled my son Hunter McClintock, of Oahu, Hawaii, and Sebastian McClintock of Lobster Cove, Maine."

Sebastian's mother turned blue from holding her breath. He could see the implications of what the lawyer just imparted—with Sebastian out of the picture, one of two things would unfold. He held his tongue waiting to see what would transpire next.

"Obviously, Hunt didn't anticipate Sebastian's early demise. As Sebastian did not have a will, then his portion of his inheritance goes to his wife."

Her mother-in-law shot out of her chair again.

"I protest." She pounded her fists on the table. "I want to contest this will. Hunt wasn't in his right mind when he made this up."

"Eugenia, I can assure you Hunt McClintock was in his right mind when he sat down with me and drew up his will. You might want to rethink your request. Why don't you have a drink of water, sit down, and let me finish."

Thankfully, the lawyer had a smidgen of control over the distraught woman. She complied, and sat back in her chair. Still, her complexion remained chalky.

"Now, as I was saying. Hunt has provided a college trust fund for Makenzie and a small annual stipend drawn from several of his stocks for Juelle in order to provide a home and family life for her and her daughter. However, there is a stipulation. If Juelle should ever remarry, she will no longer have access to the stipend, but the trust fund for Makenzie will continue until the child finishes college."

Tears formed in Juelle's eyes—he wanted to go to her, pull her into his arms, and drag her out of there. But, after the conversation they'd had yesterday at the park in regards to her bank accounts, he sensed those tears were tears of joy. She could now afford to put a purchase offer on the house on Aspen Avenue.

Eugenia found her voice. She glared at the lawyer and pointed her finger at him. "I mean it, Günter, I am contesting Hunt's will. No way is that imposter going to take over a company Hunt worked hard to make a success."

"Please. I don't want to see you get hurt by doing this, Eugenia. But if you are adamant, I have no recourse but to set in motion an action you might not want to me to take."

"I don't know what you're talking about, but I insist you abide by my request. This man is only here to collect on something he has no right to. My Sebastian is the one who gave his life for this company—took that boat out in order to make a living for the company's sake. Not that man." Her pointed finger transferred to Hunter's face.

Günter Jordan took a very deep breath, drank half the water in his tall glass, and then shuffled the papers in the folder he'd been reading from. He cleared his throat again, looked around the room, and then settled his gaze on Eugenia.

"Are you sure?"

"*Yes!*"

"Again, I caution you. You might want to reconsider."

"*Günter!*"

Hunter shook his head. When he glanced across the table at Juelle, he found her looking a bit shell-shocked at her mother-in-law's actions and caustic tone.

Günter Jordan cleared his throat, and read. "In the occasion of anticipating my wife, Eugenia, contesting my will, I request the attached note be read to those assembled." Again the lawyer cleared his throat, fidgeted with the paper he held in his hands, and then finished the water in front of him. He glanced at Eugenia, shook his head, and continued.

"My dear Eugenia," he read. "In anticipation of either you or Sebastian contesting my last requests, it is with deep disappointment that I reveal to you I am aware Sebastian is not my child. I know you were pregnant with another man's child before we were married. Although I believed him to be mine at the time, it was very evident shortly after he was born that I was not his father. By then, it was too late. I had given up everything I held dear to make a decent life for you and your son, as well as running a struggling business."

Eugenia gasped, slumped forward—her head hit the table. Juelle was around the end of the table so fast Hunter's head spun.

"Call 911," Juelle screamed. "Oh, my God. She's having a heart attack. Hunter, hurry."

Günter was at Eugenia's side in a heartbeat— before Hunter finished punching in the call on his cell phone. The lawyer drew Eugenia into his arms—his ministrations gentle. He held Eugenia against his chest while he checked for a heartbeat—his concern and distress beyond impersonal. Hunter had an idea there was more to the couple's friendship than just a business acquaintance.

Hunter ushered Juelle from the room, and out to the sidewalk to wait for the ambulance. They didn't have long to wait.

"Hi, Juelle. What's going on here?" The driver jumped from the vehicle as two paramedics opened the back doors and dragged a gurney out.

"Looks like Eugenia might have had a heart attack. She passed out." Juelle introduced Hunter to Sheila Kidman, and the two shook hands.

"Where's Eugenia?" Sheila walked to the back of the ambulance.

"She's in the conference room."

"Boy, she sure has had some bad luck lately. What happened?"

Juelle kept pace with Sheila as they followed the two paramedics."

"She's been under a lot of stress, as you know, what with Hunt dying a year ago, and now Sebastian. She got all worked up over a few of her husband's bequeaths when Mr. Jordan read Hunt's will. I hope she isn't having a heart attack."

"Well, you just stay calm now, and we'll get her checked over real fast. The hospital is just around the corner, but we'll get an EKG going as soon as we settle her in the van. I'll call ahead and they'll get the STEMI alert in place."

True to Sheila's words, they had Eugenia loaded up

in the ambulance and at the hospital, where a room was already assigned. Juelle gave the necessary information to the registration receptionist, and then rushed to Eugenia's side, leaving Mr. Jordan and him waiting outside. Juelle filled them in when she joined them in the waiting room.

"The nurse gave her an Aspirin, while someone else took blood. A team from the Cardiac Catherization Lab took over, and the same cardiology specialist who had worked on Hunt, started assessing Eugenia's condition. They gave her 4000 units of Heparin and did another EKG."

"How is she?" Mr. Jordan enquired.

"It's too early to tell, but she was awake when I left."

"That's a good sign." Hunter hoped he sounded positive. "We might just as well have a seat. Can I get anyone a coffee?"

"I'll go." Günter headed out of the small room. "Love Caters All has their truck in the parking lot today. What can I get for you?"

They gave him their orders, and then found a place to sit on the other side of the room. Juelle closed her eyes and tilted her head back against the seat.

****

Later that evening, after all the commotion at the lawyers and rushing Eugenia McClintock to the hospital, Hunter sat in the Adirondack chair outside his room at the end of the motel, and took out the letter from his father. He held it in his hand, and stared out at the receding tide as it began its journey out to sea. In the distance, white sails dotted the horizon and fishing trawlers were heading in for the evening. A mild drizzle pulled in the mist, and within a few minutes turned to a downpour. The harbor was obliterated. He shut his eyes and shot back in his chair. Did he want to read what his father had to say? Would it make any difference now? He'd had a happy childhood growing up with his mother and her family. He ran a successful travel company with her. He'd had a couple of relationships, but nothing serious enough to want to settle down and raise a family. He loved children and even wanted a few of his own—someday. He pictured Makenzie, an ideal little tyke who had stolen a piece of his heart. As had her mother. Had he become too fond of Juelle? Hell yes, he was way more than fond of her already. But she didn't need him or his baggage—the woman had enough of her own to deal with. And, thank God, that cheating S.O.B. was not his half-brother. That was one thing he didn't have to regret and was glad he'd come to Lobster Cove to discover.

He looked down at the folded envelope and shoved it back in his pocket without opening it. It didn't matter what his father had to say. It was too late. His mother was right. If nothing else, he had come to Lobster Cove to face his demons. It was time to let go of the past. He could go back to Oahu with a lighter spirit.

Being made partner with Sebastian said it all—at least his father openly acknowledged him. Like Juelle, he was beginning to feel sorry for Eugenia.

He wondered how Juelle was taking the news of the two of them being part owners of McClintock and McClintock Lobster Company, now that Sebastian was dead.

****

Juelle pulled up at Katelyn's drive and turned the

ignition off. Drained from the afternoon's shocking events, and Eugenia's near heart attack, she sat in the car for a few minutes before going inside. So much had transpired, she had a hard time grasping the impact it was going to have on her and Makenzie's life. A positive impact, for the most part.

"Oh. My. God. Girl, you look white as a ghost." Katelyn met her at the front door. "What the hell happened today? Come on in and sit down. Tell me everything. Your daughter is sleeping."

Katelyn led her to the living room where they both sat on the sofa.

"Don't you dare tell me Eugenia walked away with everything? That woman…"

"No. She got the house and a substantial financial settlement to keep her in the manner in which she has become accustomed, as they say. But I just got back from the hospital. She passed out at the lawyer's office and had to be rushed to the hospital. They suspect she had a heart attack and are keeping her overnight to run tests just to make sure."

"*Heart attack!* Holy crap! What happened at that meeting this afternoon?"

"Apparently, Sebastian isn't Hunt's son. Eugenia was pregnant with another man's baby when they got married, or very soon after. Hunt suspected as much, but kept it to himself all these years."

"Why did he spill the beans now?"

"Because Eugenia contested the will. Called Hunter a fraud. Hunt must have anticipated she would if Hunter showed up and inherited along with Sebastian. Mr. Jordan made an attempt to talk her out of it, but you know Eugenia, she persisted. He had no recourse but to honor Hunt's wishes and read the letter out loud. It was quite a shock."

"I imagine it was. How is she doing?"

"Doing okay when I left. Mr. Jordan is with her now. I think he's sweet on her."

"You're kidding, right?"

"They have been friends for a long time. I wouldn't be at all surprised."

"Oh, my God. Do you think Sebastian is Mr. Jordan's son?

"No. I don't think he would have read that letter if he was."

"I don't know. If he's sweet on her, maybe he was ready for her to acknowledge his paternity."

"I didn't get the feeling they were hiding anything."

"Well, at least you won't have to face Eugenia tonight. What about Hunter? How did he take the news that he doesn't have a half-brother after all?"

"He was real cool about it all, even drove to the hospital with us. Mr. Jordan handed him a sealed envelope from his father before Eugenia's attack."

"OMG. How mysteriously old world. Wonder what it said? Did he read it aloud?"

"No. He wasn't instructed to open it in front of everyone."

"What about you? Did you inherit anything?"

"Let's just say I'll have the finances to make a solid purchase offer on the house on Aspen Avenue. I hope Jessica hasn't accepted anyone else's offer yet. I'll contact her first thing in the morning. "

"How exciting. I'm so happy for you." Katelyn leaned over and hugged her. "We're going to have to do some furniture shopping."

"I'm not finished. Ready for this? Hunter and I are now the proud joint owners of McClintock and McClintock Lobster Company."

"Okay, now that's a shocker. No wonder Eugenia had a heart attack. Besides being found out about Sebastian, she is about to lose her prominent standing in the community. This calls for a celebration. I think I have some wine in the kitchen somewhere."

"I'd love to indulge, but I have to drive Makenzie home."

"Makenzie is sound asleep for the night. Leave her here. You've had enough to deal with for one day. Go home. Relax."

"When are you and Sven going to get married and have children of your own? You've practically adopted my daughter as it is. You'd make a fantastic mother."

"You know we aren't officially engaged, so of course we haven't set a date yet. I think he's dragging his feet." Katelyn jumped from the sofa and headed for the kitchen. "One glass of wine. It will relax you enough so you can get a good night's sleep."

Juelle followed her friend to the kitchen. She sat at the table while Katelyn poured the wine, then handed her a glass.

"To a new lease on life. May you have nothing but happy days ahead."

They tapped glasses, sipped, and looked at each other, then burst out laughing.

"I know it's not funny, but I have a bunch of fluttering butterflies tickling my insides."

"You so deserve this."

"I'm not sure. And I'm not sure I'm going to keep

my portion of the business. Hunter and I will have to put our heads together and work it out."

"Do you think he'll stay in Lobster Cove and run the company?"

"He has his own business to manage back in Hawaii. I can't see him giving all that up to live in Maine. Who would want to give up all that tropical paradise? If it was me, and I lived in Oahu all my life, I'd be hard pressed to give it all up."

Two glasses of celebratory wine later, Juelle eased her car into the garage and was about to lower the door, when a car pulled up behind her. Hunter got out and walked toward her. His short sleeved, royal-blue golf shirt showed off his muscular biceps and hugged his waistline. His snug tan slacks accentuated his assets, his dark hair was tousled, and his expression hard to read as he ambled her way. He was definitely one desirable man who had kissing down to an art. And if she didn't get those thoughts out of her head right this minute, she was going to be in big trouble.

"What are you doing here?"

"I was on my way to get something to eat and decided to stop by to make sure you were all right. See if there was anything I could do for you."

There were a few things she could think of, but none of them were appropriate, considering she hadn't known him long and had just buried her husband.

"I'm fine, thanks. But ready to call it a night. Would you like to come in for coffee?"

"Do you need help carrying Makenzie in the house?"

"She's spending the night at Katelyn's. She was already asleep and Katelyn offered."

"Have you had dinner? Would you care to join me? I was heading to The Cliffside."

It might be the wine talking, but she didn't want to be alone. And she and Hunter had business to discuss.

"Give me a minute to freshen up." She walked up to the front door and invited Hunter in.

"I'll wait outside, if you don't mind. Somehow I don't think Eugenia would appreciate knowing I've been inside her home. Especially after the reading of Hunt's will."

"It's my home as well."

"Still, I prefer to wait out here."

"I'll just be a moment."

When they arrived at The Cliffside, an upscale restaurant perched on the cliff overlooking Frenchman Bay, they were ushered to a secluded corner table next to a window overlooking the lights on the harbor. Soft dinner music played in the background and a candle flickered in the center of the table. The romantic ambiance not lost on Juelle. The two glasses of wine she'd consumed at Katelyn's had gone straight to her head, not to mention she was sitting across from the very appealing Hunter McClintock, without feeling one bit guilty.

Hunter ordered wine, and a full lobster dinner special for two. Once the wine was poured, Hunter lifted his glass and held it out across the table. She lifted her glass and clicked the edge against his in a salute.

"To our potential joint adventure."

Juelle pulled back, and locked eyes with him. "I told you I'm not sure I want any part of the company."

"Be patient. We'll work it out. After the run-in

with Eugenia that first day at the hospital, I decided I needed to prove her wrong and made up my mind to have a DNA test in anticipation of there being a problem with the McClintock family. I mentioned it to Mr. Jordan and he suggested I also request DNA from Sebastian. No doubt he suspected what was in Hunt's letter to Eugenia, should she contest the will. We had the test performed the day I stopped at the hospital to see Sebastian. I hope this will put an end to Eugenia's claim that I'm not Hunt's son and prove I'm not a fake. As soon as the results come in, they are to be sent to Mr. Jordan."

"Anyone would have to be blind not to look at you and think you aren't Hunt's son. You're the spitting image of your father when he was younger. You don't have to do any of this for my sake, or to feel legitimate in order to take over the helm at McClintock and McClintock."

"Thank you. It's encouraging to hear you believe me."

"Of course, I believe you. And now that Mr. Jordan read the letter from Hunt, it isn't hard for me to believe Sebastian wasn't his son."

"Your mother-in-law kept it from her husband. It had to be a shock for her to discover he was aware of her secret all along. As for the company, I talked to Mr. Jordan while we were at the hospital. He is expediting the contents of Hunt's will, as well as waiting on results of the DNA tests. We should have confirmation one way or another in a couple days."

He looked at her with those sexy sable eyes—her insides melted. She took another sip of wine and wished their main course would arrive soon. The wine was going to her head and she was starting to have serious feelings for Hunter—feelings she had no business feeling.

Saved by the waitress arriving at that exact moment, she put her glass down and sat back while the steaming platter was placed in front of her—a whole lobster placed on top of a bowl filled with scallops, clams, potatoes, and corn on the cob. Juelle didn't hesitate, she dug into the lobster tail, swirled a forkful of the sweet white meat into a dish of melted butter and brought it to her lips. The silence from across the table made her nervous. She looked up to find Hunter McClintock staring at her lips. She flicked her tongue over them and wiped the butter off with her napkin. He shifted in his seat and shadowed her movements of a second ago, and dunked his lobster in the butter, and then brought it to his mouth. Butter dribbled down his chin. Juelle's hand shot out to wipe it off, but she caught herself just in time, and put them in her lap. His eyes followed her hands, and then looked up in to her eyes as he took his own napkin and swiped at the butter. Her insides moaned. Having dinner with Hunter was too erotic by far, not to mention a big mistake. At least they were in a public place. If they weren't, she was sure she'd be making a complete fool of herself over him. There was no way she was getting involved with Hunter McClintock. No way.

He cleared his throat, chewed another piece of lobster, and washed it down with wine.

"We need to go check out the business—see if it's something we might want to consider. How about tomorrow?"

The man was full of surprises tonight. "Do you

know anything about the lobster business?"

"No. But I do know how to run a business. How hard can it be? Do you think Katelyn will watch Makenzie a little longer tomorrow morning so we can meet with Coleman Baker? I understand he's the acting manager."

"I'm…"

"You are part owner—at least for now. I'll pick you up at ten."

"I'll give her a call in the morning. It's getting late, I should be going."

"No dessert?"

"No room. The meal was delicious. Thank you."

Hunter paid the bill, and ushered her out the door into the balmy evening. When they were buckled into their seats, he started the car and drove past the McClintock Estate.

"Wait a minute. You just passed the drive to the estate."

"I'm sorry. I thought we'd go watch the sunset up on Cadillac Mountain. I hear it's spectacular, and it's such a lovely night. If you'd rather not, just say so. I'm so used to planning and arranging trips and events I wasn't thinking—it's the travel agent in me."

Juelle settled back in her seat. What would it hurt if they drove back up to the top of the mountain? Hunter was right. It was a spectacular evening to watch the sunset.

"Thanks. I'd love to."

When they reached the summit, they climbed out of the car and walked out to the center of the of granite rock, turned and watched the evening colors of pink, purple, with a few puffy clouds melding into the sunset.

The sun's decent put on a spectacular evening performance for those assembled. Hunter put his arm around her and pulled her close. She didn't resist. Being in his arms was like coming home—safe, secure. Her heart raced, his scent filled her with desire. She tried to step away, he held on. Heat ignited at his touch. She gave in and remained in his arms while the sun dipped over the horizon and the air cooled.

He walked her to the car, and before she knew it his hands cupped her face and his lips laid claim to her willing mouth. Their breaths mingled, and she clung to him, not able to get close enough—her emotions on fire. Juelle didn't know what she had ever done in her lifetime to deserve someone like Hunter McClintock to show up on her doorstep in her time of need. Sure, she had Katelyn, whose shoulder she'd cried on, divulged all her deepest, darkest secrets, and who had been there since day one—her first friend in Lobster Cove. But Katelyn was no substitute for being held in warm, secure, protective male arms—like Hunter's. His kisses had melted her frozen heart and warmed her insides like no one else had—including Sebastian. His closeness raised her blood pressure to fever pitch and ignited dormant emotions she'd repressed over the past year. Could he feel what he did to her? Did he think she was easy? Needy?

Hopeless?

"Let's get out of here," he whispered against her lips, his breath sending exotic quivers to her center.

She could only agree.

****

In what seemed like hours, but was the shortest ride down the mountain ever, Hunter had his car pulled up next to the Frenchman Bay Motel. She was in his arms as soon as he turned off the motor. His kiss was meant to assure her he was still interested. Her response answered his call.

Hunter had Juelle out of the car, down the veranda, and inside his hotel room before she could change her mind. He'd been going crazy since he'd met her, and he didn't think he could keep his hands off her another minute. He unlocked the door, kicked it behind them, and frog-marched her directly to the bed, his lips locked on hers the entire time.

Her arms clung to him in a hold destined to tie them together forever. The way her body moved his, there was no way he could hold back. The passion in her embrace was his undoing. He slipped his hands up under her top, felt her heart beat quicken as his hand molded her breasts. Good God, they fit his hand so perfectly. And Lord, was that her leg that just wrapped around his leg pulling him closer.

He stopped long enough to unbutton her blouse and slide it down around her sexy body. He lowered his face and snuggled into her neck, kissing his way down to the cleavage he'd explored moments before. Her arms yanked on his shirt, he helped her remove it, and thank God, they were both naked and laying on the bed so he could make love to her.

Hunter looked into Juelle's eyes, making sure she was aware of what they were about to do. He had no doubts this was the right thing for him. Her thoroughly kissed lips smiled up at him. Her fingers rubbed across his mouth, down his neck, and headed south to his navel, belt buckle, zipper, and beyond. God help him, he was lost. It was the sign he was looking for. His own hands found their way down her delectable, sexy body, and hugged her hips close to his aching need. Between the two of them, he wasn't sure who was needier, but then, it didn't matter. His hand found her center. She arched into him. He slide his hand back up to encompass her breast and positioned himself over her, levering his body mere centimeters from hers. She wrapped her legs around his hips and pulled him down to her. God help him, they were destined to reach this moment in time. Together, they made love, both reaching a climax that had them out of breath, yet sated, and entwined and clinging to each other. He wanted more.

"That was…"

"Perfect. You're perfect."

"I don't know what to say."

"Nothing. Just lay here in my arms."

"I should go."

"Stay. I don't want you to leave yet. I'm not sure I can ever let you go. At least not tonight."

"Hunter…"

"Shhhh. Relax. You don't have to rush home tonight. We'll deal with everything tomorrow."

She snuggled in his arms and fell asleep. Hunter watched her breathing relax, soaked in her beauty, the way her eyelashes swept over her soft cheeks now full of color, her lips swollen, and he wanted her again. How was he ever going to leave her behind when he went back to Hawaii? He'd fallen in love with an angel.

Chapter Ten

Hunter met Juelle at Pier One the following morning, and together they entered the offices of McClintock and McClintock. He held the door open, smiled down at her pensive face, and gave her a brief hug and a peck on the forehead.

"It's only a consultation. Nothing saying we have to keep the business. But it won't hurt to check it out."

She hesitated, looked uncomfortable. Damn. He didn't want her to have any regrets about last night, but it was obvious from her shyness she was having second thoughts.

"If you want the company, I'll sell my portion to you. I don't know a thing about the lobster business." Her eyes lowered, her voice a whisper. She scanned the area as if she'd never been inside the warehouse.

He panned the ample entranceway and discovered the door to the left stood open.

"We'll see. Wait until we talk to Mr. Baker, find out what shape the company is in, then we'll talk."

He escorted her into the room that served as a reception area, as well as a work space. Coleman Baker sat behind a long, low counter that served as a desk, which held what looked like the latest in computer technology. Behind him, along the back wall, was other electrical equipment he surmised monitored the weather conditions, water temperatures, and video equipment which appeared to be currently supervising activity in the warehouse and the holding tanks.

McClintock's acting manager stood and extended his hand in welcome. Hunter stepped forward and clasped the man's hand. Juelle followed suit.

"Thanks for seeing us, Mr. Baker. I hope we aren't imposing on your workday."

"Not at all. Call me Cole. It's good to see a McClintock show some interest in the family business."

Hunter could only surmise who he referred to, but didn't offer his own take on the subject. Or on Sebastian. Once again he was thankful that even if others didn't know it yet, he was happy to learn Sebastian was not his half-brother—not a real McClintock.

"As you've already heard, Juelle and I are now co-owners of the company. Although I don't claim to know much about the lobster business, I do know about running a company. We'd appreciate it if you would run us through the main points of this one, first of which is, how viable is the business? Is it turning a profit?"

"Good place to start. Yes. It was a bit iffy after Hunt died. Things started going downhill, but we're back on track now. How about a tour while we talk. It might give you a broader picture of our operations." He clicked off a few controls, grabbed a set of keys, and escorted them out into the hall before locking the door behind them. "It's never a good idea to leave such expensive equipment unattended. Not saying we're worried about the competition, but in this day and age, you never know." The man grinned and started walking down the hallway. "Follow me."

He led them down a narrow hall and opened a door leading into an elongated warehouse. Large aerated tanks lined both sides of the spacious room, the temperature cool, the scent of seawater and marine life, heavy.

"This is our holding facility. We've upgraded our systems to chill the water temperature to 36 degrees in the tanks, which puts the lobster to 'sleep', so to speak. This allows for better quality and taste—it locks in the freshness. We also have a water filtration system to simulate the lobster's natural environs, also helps maintain their freshness before we ship out and during shipment."

"How do you keep them fresh when you ship them?" Juelle rubbed her bare arms. The air in the warehouse was cool due to the temperature of the holding tanks. Hunter wanted to put his arms around her, warm her, but this wasn't the place. He didn't want rumors to run rampant about her so soon after her husband's funeral.

"We ship with cold packs. Keeps them cool until they arrive at their destination." Cole called to a man who was at the far end of the building leaning over one of the tanks. "Jim. Got a minute?"

A man with a five o'clock shadow, looking to be in his fifty's, ambled over.

"This is Jim Sherman, our tank room manager. He oversees the grading process. This is Hunter McClintock and Juelle, Sebastian's widow."

"Pleased to meet you." He shook their hands and stepped back. "How can I help you?"

"They're here to find out a bit about our operation."

"Well, we have a quality control team—five of the most experienced lobster men in town. Hard to explain the control process—experience is the key. These men know a thing or two about lobsters. They've been at it a long time. McClintock's is lucky to have them."

They finished checking out the tanks, then walked out into the bright sunshine and a comfortable breeze blowing in off the harbor, and stepped up on to the pier to check out the fleet. McClintock's had two trawlers tied up at the pier at the moment. But harbor life thrived—the area was afloat with kayaks, sailboats, and in the distance, a cruise ship tendering in passengers near Bar Harbor. Pier Two, across the way, was a teeming mass of activity, with tourists and locals visiting the vendors and carts lined up along the midway, part of the Oil and Water Art Festival that was underway.

"Most of our fleet left early this morning and haven't returned yet. We maintain a fleet of fifteen," Cole stated. "Our captains are experienced and dependable, and our trawlers are equipped with the latest technology. We employ a few private fishermen during our busy season. McClintock's have secured the rights for several of the fishing areas."

"Impressive. What about pay? Benefits for the employees?"

"The price per pound right now is significant. With our catch and sales on a daily basis, there is no reason our fishermen have to be underpaid. We provide benefits and health insurance, as well. If you'd like to see the books, I can arrange that."

"Who deals with the financial end of the business?"

"You're looking at him." Cole smiled, pointing his thumb to his chest. "Hunt promoted me before his death. Sebastian had his say until the accident, but he wasn't keen on the business end of the company—he liked to be out on the water, so I stepped in and made sure everything was back on track. You aiming to sell this company? Or take it over?"

Hunter admired the man's forthright manner. The question was, did he intend to take over? It was something he and Juelle needed to discuss further.

"It isn't necessary to see the books just yet. As for taking over the company, that remains to be seen. Juelle and I need to discuss our options first. In the meantime, we'd be happy for you to continue in your managing capacity. Is there someone you can suggest to assist you. It looks to me as if you have a lot on your plate at the moment."

"Yes. I have someone who has been working with me. He's an honest man. I'm sure he'd be happy to continue."

"I'll get back with you as soon as we discuss the situation and make a decision." He faced Juelle. "Does that work for you?"

"Of course. Thank you, Mr. Baker. Like Hunter said, we'll be in touch."

They left Pier One and headed toward their individual vehicles.

"We can go to the park and discuss this over a cup of coffee, or, we can go somewhere else where we'll have more privacy."

"It's rather crowded there right now with the festival in full swing. Feel up for a walk? There's a trail along the shore down the coast, or we can follow one of the trails in Acadia."

"It sounds like just what we need."

The shaded woodland trail they chose was a flat, easy trek. They strolled in silence, side by side. Juelle's heart raced at Hunter's closeness. Maybe the park would have been a safer choice to have that talk. She hadn't forgotten their lovemaking the night before, how he'd made her toes tingle, her heart race. Hunter was an excellent lover, she hadn't wanted to leave his arms, but she knew what they shared wasn't going to last. How could it? He wasn't going to hang around Lobster Cove. They'd both been caught up in the McClintock web, and in every instance he'd championed her side. Not that she'd declared sides, but it was comforting to have someone who understood the hurt. Because there was no doubt Hunter McClintock still hurt from his father's desertion. She had to guard her heart against more heartache at the McClintock hands. Business or no business, Hunter had his own travel agency to run back in Hawaii.

She picked up the pace to match her racing mind and heart. Hunter clasped her hand and tugged, causing her steps to slow. His touch zinged right through to her heart. Maybe this walk along a secluded path wasn't such a good idea after all.

"Penny for them?" His words low, sexy, held a touch of humor.

"I suspect my thoughts are the same as yours."

"You'd be surprised what I'm thinking."

He tugged on her hands, squeezed her fingers, and pulled her to his side. Oh, my God. The man was lethal. Her cheeks warmed. She lowered her head to hide the results of what his touch did to her, let alone the meaning his words invoked. She had to remind herself he wasn't a permanent fixture in the Cove.

"I'm serious. I'm not sure I'm up to running a business—let alone an international business the size of McClintock's. What about you? Are you ready to live here in Lobster Cove and take over your father's affairs?"

"Not really."

She knew it. He confirmed it—he wasn't staying. She'd been a fool to let him make love to her.

"Taking over the business requires serious deliberation. Cole has things under control and doing an excellent job. How hard would it be to promote him, give him a raise, and keep the company running as is until we decide what we want to do?"

"What are you proposing?"

She stopped and swung around to face him, their hands still entwined. The lopsided grin and raised eyebrows suggested his feelings were the same as hers right now. She wriggled her hands out of his and walked down the trail. She couldn't think while his touch sent the wrong signals to her brain via her heart. A few birds flittered in and out of the trees. A squirrel scampered up a tree trunk. Two bikes whizzed by, their peddlers nodding a hello as they passed.

"Juelle. I'm sorry." He caught up to her. "I know you don't want to hear this, but I've been going crazy thinking about our making love last night. You know I've become fond of you and Makenzie. I think you feel the same way."

He swung her around to face him again. She couldn't form a single word as she looked into his dark sable eyes—eyes looking right back into her very soul.

She froze as his lips laid claim to hers. Her insides melted and she clung to him, and kissed him right back—she didn't care. She arched into his hold—couldn't get close enough. His arms spanned her hips, his hands tugged her into his hard arousal.

"It's too bad we aren't behind closed doors right now." His whispered words fanned against her mouth were erotic. Her insides turned to mush.

It took a minute for sanity to put in an appearance. She stepped back, not letting go of him—her arms clinging. He was more than physically fit, he was desirable from head to toe. She cleared her throat, and looked into smoldering eyes that made her want to jump back into his arms. The McClintocks hadn't been good to her. Would he be any different? The taste of his lips on hers had her mind in turmoil. She couldn't think of anything else but Hunter. His arms around her. But she had to shake those sensual emotions out of her system. There was much more at stake here than worrying about the man's kisses. She didn't need another broken heart. And Lord help her, she was falling for him. Hard.

"Sebastian has only been—"

"Forget Sebastian. I have. He's not my half-brother. I won't let you down like he did. You can count on me."

Doubts and confusion set in. Was he right? Was Hunt McClintock not Sebastian's father, as Hunt had stated in his letter? Would the DNA test prove otherwise? Sebastian had been her husband. Not a very good one, but her husband, nevertheless. There was no erasing that fact. A smidgen of guilt over Hunter's erotic lovemaking the night before washed over her.

"Look, let's sit down on that bench up ahead and talk this through like we planned."

He ran his hand over his face, through his thick dark hair. Her heart thudded. Without touching her, he walked up ahead and sat down, waiting for her to do the same.

She had to shake off the sexual fantasy she'd been having in his arms, which was driving her crazy. A relationship with Hunter McClintock would end up going nowhere. Why he bothered coming on to her, making love to her and stirring up emotions better left alone, was a puzzle she didn't want to unravel.

"Here's what I'm thinking." He slung his arm over the back of the bench as she sat down, keeping a space between them.

He couldn't be as affected by their lovemaking as she'd been if he could switch to business so casually.

"If we decide to hang on to the business, it can only be a win-win for both of us. You won't have to worry about a job to provide for you and Makenzie, unless you want to get involved in the business. You'll have a steady income and collateral to purchase the house we looked at the other day. I can continue with my business back home. If we find it isn't working for either of us, we can do one of two things. Either one of us can buy the other out, or we can sell the company to an interested buyer. I suggest we take a wait and see attitude, until things settle down."

She had to admit he had a point. She could stay at home and raise Makenzie, and re-evaluate her options once her daughter started school, as she had contemplated.

"It doesn't seem right to own a company and not

be involved."

"Give it some time. Make an appointment with the realtor to seal the deal on the house, first. Talk to Mr. Jordan. He can help with all the legal details pertaining to Sebastian's affairs. In the meantime, I'm going to meet with Cole and go over the financial records. You can join me if you wish."

"No, you can meet with him on your own. I'll pick up Makenzie from Katelyn's, talk to Mr. Jordan, and give the realtor a call. I want to call the hospital and see how Eugenia is doing. She appeared to be doing much better when I called this morning, but I want to visit and make sure."

She could only hope something positive would come out of the session with the lawyer this afternoon. She was anxious to leave the McClintock Estate behind. And start putting distance between her and Hunter.

****

Katelyn brought Makenzie to the park to meet Juelle. She found her friend feeding her daughter a vanilla ice cream cone, the two of them were sitting on a bench in the gazebo out of the hot afternoon sun and away from the mingling festival crowd. Makenzie started to wiggle off the bench when she saw her. Juelle rushed forward and caught her up in a hug before the baby managed to fall.

"How's the lobster business? You and Hunter going to remain partners?" Her friend bit into what was left of the melting cone.

Juelle shook her head. "I don't know, Katelyn. It all sounds too good to be true. And you know how that goes."

"If it's too good to be true, then it probably isn't

good."

"Hunter thinks we should take a wait and see attitude. And it does sound like a solid plan. But I have to talk to Mr. Jordan first and double check my finances—make sure everything is in order, and that becoming partners with Hunter is in my best interest."

"Honey, becoming partners with Hunter sounds like the epitome of perfect."

"Yes, well, he's not sticking around Lobster Cove, so any relationship, even a minor one with him, is not a good idea."

Makenzie anchored her hands on either side of Juelle's face and pivoted her head around and planted a vanilla kiss on her mouth. All three broke out laughing.

"Here. Have a wet cloth." Katelyn handed her a fresh wipe. Juelle cleaned up her daughter first, and then mopped up her own cheeks and lips.

"Thanks for taking care of Makenzie—again. If this keeps up, I'm going to have to put you on the payroll."

"I won't take a dime. But once classes begin in September, I won't be available."

"I'm going to look into a day care center, even if it's part time. Any suggestions?"

"Jolene Graham is the director at Hearts and Hands. I understand she takes children starting at six months old, so that should work for you. But, hey, I'll watch this little miss anytime in between, you know I love having her."

"Thanks. Once things get back to normal, whatever normal is, I might need an occasional babysitter. In the meantime, I have to meet with Jessica Martin to seal the deal on the house, sign the papers, and get through a closing. Once all that is done, we'll get together and do some furniture shopping."

"Exciting. Let me know when, and I'll make time."

****

Juelle met with Günter Jordan in the afternoon, who assured her there would be no problem purchasing the house on Aspen Avenue. In fact, her finances were such that she didn't need a loan and could purchase the property outright. She called Jessica Martin again to set up a meeting to take care of all the arrangements.

"I did have an anonymous offer on the house a couple hours after you left the other day," Jessica told her over the phone. "I put him off—told the gentleman I was waiting to hear back from you. I'll give him a call and tell him the house is no longer on the market."

"Thank you, Jessica. You don't know how much I appreciate your help. Mr. Jordan will be working with you to take care of all the details. In the meantime, I'd like to look at the house again, if it isn't too much trouble."

"Not at all. Stop by and I'll give you the key. You can go when it suits you."

Later, Juelle drove to the hospital to check in on Eugenia. She walked in to find her mother-in-law sitting up in bed, refreshing her makeup and combing her hair.

"You're looking much better. How are you feeling?"

Her mother-in-law gathered the assorted cosmetics strewn across the hospital table and shoved them into the large case Juelle had dropped off for her earlier, along with other items Eugenia requested. Her mother-in-law lowered her eyes, as if she'd been caught doing something illegal. Eugenia didn't go anywhere without first applying a full coat of makeup. Not that she overdid—the woman wore it without looking like a made up tart—Eugenia's own words.

Juelle hefted Makenzie higher up on her hip.

"As you can see I'm fine. In fact, they plan to release me tomorrow morning. I'll be able to attend the Chamber of Commerce Meeting in the afternoon."

"Do you think that wise? Maybe you should take a few more days to rest before jumping back in to your projects."

"I can handle it. It wasn't my heart, after all. Just some silly indigestion and a bit of stress acting like a heart attack."

"You have been under a lot of stress, Eugenia. I'm sure the doctors have told you to get more rest."

"Nevertheless, I'm chairing the Lobster Crawl this year and it's important I be there tomorrow to give an update. I can't let them down."

Juelle shifted Makenzie, who started to nod off from boredom. She wasn't about to remind Eugenia that if the chamber had their way, she wouldn't be chairing anything connected with the Lobster Crawl the end of August, let alone the chamber itself.

"I've made an offer on a house out on Aspen Avenue. Mr. Jordan has agreed to handle everything for me."

"Günter will be thorough. If he doesn't think you should buy it, he'll tell you. And that will be the end of it." She set the table aside and straightened the sheets with her hands, folding the top over, then smoothing it one last time. She laid her hands on top and rested her head on the piles of pillows stacked behind her back.

Well, that went easier than she'd anticipated. Eugenia appeared calmer, almost friendly. Maybe the near heart attack episode had a silver lining, and Eugenia was turning over a new leaf.

About to say her goodbyes, Juelle stood speechless as Günter Jordan walked in the room, a large bouquet of red roses in his hand. He paused just inside, glanced at Eugenia, and then Juelle.

"I see our patient is doing well," he said, breaking the tension in the room.

"I was just leaving. It's time to put Makenzie in bed for the night."

Juelle made her way down the corridor, a smile on her lips at the turn of events. It appeared Günter Jordan was sweet on Eugenia? Was Eugenia sweet on Günter Jordan?

My, my, only time would tell.

****

Günter handed Eugenia long stemmed yellow roses wrapped in tissue paper.

"I stopped by Flowers in Bloom. Inge Olson said a fresh shipment just arrived—said you'd like these."

"They are exquisite. I'll have one of the nurses get a vase and put them in water." She sniffed the blooms, and then laid them down on the bed in front of her.

"You look much better today. How are you feeling?"

"It was just a scare, but I'll be out of here sometime tomorrow. All I needed was a bit of rest. I'm so sorry I overreacted, Günter. It was as if my whole world was falling apart when you read Hunt's letter. I had no idea Hunt knew, and still he stayed with me all those years, never saying a word."

"I'm sorry Eugenia. I know how hard this has been on you. You've been under a lot of strain."

"You have to understand, Günter, I didn't want Sebastian to know Hunt wasn't his real father. I wanted stability for my son. Stability I never had growing up."

"And Hunt treated him like his own son. It's over, my dear. Sebastian is gone."

Tears filled her eyes. "It's not that easy. He was my whole life."

"I know. But you need to let it all go, now. In fact, I've been meaning to talk to you since Hunt passed. And now the formalities of his will have been taken care of, I wondered if you'd like to have dinner with me? After they release you from the hospital, that is."

"Günter! Are you asking me out on a date?"

"It's only a dinner date, Eugenia. We've been friends a long time. Both of us are unencumbered, now. It would be appropriate to see other people on occasion. That is, if you are so inclined?"

She didn't need to think it over. Günter Jordan was a fine, upstanding citizen. His work ethics were beyond reproach.

"Yes. I'd love to have dinner with you."

"Good. Now that that's settled, what do you know about a young man and his two children, who have been vacationing close by—a Mr. Cavanaugh? I understand he's a Boston lawyer."

"The name sounds familiar, but I can't place him."

"Keep an ear open. I've hired a paralegal and thinking of expanding the firm further—hiring someone to take on part of my clients so I can free up my time. I'm not getting any younger."

"You're not old."

"Do you ever feel as if you've wasted your whole life taking care of everyone else's problems and you don't have time for yourself?"

"I've enjoyed helping others in the community."

"And you've done an admirable job. However, it's about time someone else took over—let the younger generation take on the responsibility of running things."

"It's my whole life. What would I do?"

"Travel. Haven't you ever wondered what was down the road? Around the bend? In the next state?"

"I never stopped to think about it."

"Well, think about it while you're lying in that bed tonight. Between the both of us, we have the time, the finances, and each other. And we're not getting any younger."

Chapter Eleven

Juelle entered the building with Makenzie in tow and found a seat close to the exit in case she needed to take a cranky baby out of the meeting. She greeted several members who were there to attend the Lobster Cove Chamber of Commerce meeting. Makenzie was her usual happy self, and was content to sit and play with her toys on her special floor mat as the meeting got underway.

Paul Varner, a tall, sturdy stern, big-time marketing guy originally from Boston, and Executive Director of the Chamber, opened the meeting, followed by the secretary reading minutes and the treasurer's report. The floor was opened to Old Business. Juelle waited anxiously while other matters were addressed before the issue of membership was presented. She observed Eugenia from the corner of her eye. Not surprising, she sat two rows up to the right on the edge of her seat, next to Günter Jordan. Eugenia shouldn't even be here—she should be home resting after just being released from the hospital. For sure the meeting would be stressful. God forbid if she had a real heart attack. Knowing what was about to transpire, Juelle swung her foot nervously, and waited.

"On the issue of membership," Paul stated. "We have a few pending applications and two special memberships needing more discussion before we can make a sound decision."

Juelle stood and asked for privilege of the floor before she lost her nerve, and before anyone else had a chance to speak.

"The board recognizes Juelle McClintock." The chairman pounded his gavel and nodded in her direction.

A hush fell over the room. Juelle suspected their anticipation in what she had to say was due to her recent loss of her husband, the rumors in regard to Nora Spears and Sebastian's affair, Eugenia's heart attack scare, and the status of McClintock and McClintock. She hoped they hadn't discovered Sebastian wasn't Hunt's son.

"I know the chamber is in the process of reviewing the McClintock memberships. With that in mind, I'd like to address the issue of our standing. While Eugenia is no longer connected with McClintock's business, as you have already surmised would happen, she has exemplified service to this organization for many years, as well as other organizations within the community."

"I can speak for myself." Eugenia stood, the folding chair she'd been sitting in teetered backward. Günter steadied the chair, held it in place while her mother-in-law faced the head table of attentive officers glaring back at her. "I don't need anyone speaking on my behalf."

Juelle cringed. Paul pounded the gavel on the wooden pad again.

"Please, Eugenia. Have a seat and let your daughter-in-law finish."

"Well," Eugenia huffed. And sat. Günter leaned over and whispered something in her ear.

Juelle's heart ached for her—the woman's world was falling apart around her, even though she was well taken care of by her deceased husband—who had been very generous despite the cruel deception she'd play on him all these years. Regardless, she thought Eugenia deserved better from this group. And it looked as if Günter Jordan was going to be there to help her out.

"As you say, she no longer has contacts with the business, so her membership is rightfully in question."

She wasn't sure which board member had spoken, her attention focused on Eugenia. It didn't matter. She was going to have her say.

"I understand. But as you, and everyone else here knows, Eugenia has financially supported and initiated many projects, of not only the chamber's, but other organizations in the area such as the McClintock Scholarship Award, the Fisherman's Bereavement Fund, and the Chamber's own Small Business Start-Up Fund. Without her support, many of Lobster Cove's projects would not have come to fruition."

"This is preposterous." Eugenia jumped up again, and this time pointed her finger at the board members sitting at the table in the front of the room. "I'm one of the founding members of this chamber. I organized the first meeting in order to boost the business climate and economy right here in Lobster Cove."

The room hushed in stunned silence and remained rooted to their seats throughout her outburst not wanting to miss a word. Waiting for her to continue, all eyebrows rose in surprise as she stormed out of the room. Juelle wanted to go after her to make sure she was okay, but the Board needed to be convinced.

"If you terminate her membership, you will be

doing a great injustice and disservice to the town and the chamber," Juelle said. "Eugenia might be a difficult person to deal with some of the time, but she has the town's best interest at heart and has been a hard worker no matter the project. At least consider her for a non-voting member. Or even a lifetime membership without voting privileges."

Surprised at her own gumption to stand up in front of the entire town's business community members and take a stance on Eugenia's behalf, she was pleased when Jessica Martin stood, faced her, and with a wide grin, championed her cause.

"I agree with Juelle. I make a motion the board consider Eugenia McClintock to receive lifetime membership without voting privileges."

"Do I hear a second?" Paul banged the gavel.

Five people, including Maya Cruz from Love Caters All, Tomas Darling owner of Merlots Wine Bar, Beatrice O'Brien of Sweet Bea's, and Roark Sullivan of Mariner's Fish Fry all raised their hands and shouted 'I second the motion,' simultaneously.

"I only need one," Paul called out. "Roark? How about it?"

"Yes, sir. I second the motion." Roark Sullivan tipped his head at Juelle, a devilish Irish grin on his face.

Juelle returned the smile and sat down. She looked down at her daughter and was pleased to see Makenzie still enthralled with her toys. She spotted Günter Jordan quietly slip out of the room.

Paul pounded his gavel with relish—the man had a fetish for pounding the retched thing. The good news, however, was the vote was unanimous. The room burst into applause.

"If there are no other membership issues," Paul paused, waiting for others to speak.

Juelle wasn't about to mention the possibility of membership for the new owners of McClintock and McClintock. She and Hunter still needed to come to terms with their partnership.

Paul hit the pad one more time. "Okay, then, let's move on to this year's proposed Lobster Crawl. Keep in mind we have to tie up loose ends soon. There are two more months before the event, and we have to get press releases out as soon as possible. Can we have the report from the committee chair?"

The room settled down. Everyone waited, looked around the room for someone to stand up and give a report, and then realized it was Eugenia who was instrumental in heading up the committee. A few nervous laughs broke out in the back of the room. Paul cleared his throat and pounded his gavel.

"Perhaps we should open the floor for suggestions. I believe a chowder cook-off competition at the park was suggested?"

"I think we should have an 'anything lobster' event. Doesn't need to be a competition."

"I was thinking about having sugar cookies in the shape of lobsters. Or maybe a clam and lobster chowder in a sourdough bread bowl," Julie from Julie's Coffee and Sweet Shop said.

"Lobster burgers from Maggie's Dinner," someone spoke up. "Can't beat'em."

"Don't forget we need to include the independent vendors along Pier Two."

Juelle figured Eugenia's absence was a good thing

at the moment. It gave those attending the meeting a chance to speak up about their own ideas without her mother-in-law squelching their suggestions. It was time for a younger crowd to have a say—take over.

It was also time to leave before the meeting ended and everyone started asking questions, or offering condolences. She picked up Makenzie, along with her toys, and made a quiet exit. Once on the street, she headed for her car, only to find Hunter leaning against it, his eyes following her movements. He stepped away from the vehicle when she drew near.

"Are you okay? Is Eugenia okay? I caught her and Günter Jordan leaving earlier. She looked a little pale, and a lot unhappy. Is the meeting over already?"

"No. I decided to sneak out before refreshments. I didn't feel like hanging around and being the recipient of condolences. As for Eugenia leaving, I don't blame her. She's been a staunch supporter of everything Lobster Cove, despite her sour personality. However, if she'd have stayed, she would have seen she has supporters of her own. The members stood by her—the vote was unanimous. They voted her a life-time membership. Of course, it comes without voting privileges. I'm sure she'll have something to say about that."

"What about your membership?"

"It wasn't mentioned and I didn't bring it up. I'm not sure it's relevant right now."

"About that. I talked to my mother this morning. She doesn't want Hunt's money. She suggested I talk to you about an idea she's been mulling over. Got a minute?"

"I need to feed Makenzie first, and then take

another look at the house. Jessica gave me a key."

"How about we meet there at five o'clock? I'll pick up a picnic dinner from Mariner's and we can celebrate you buying the house. We'll picnic in the backyard."

She didn't think it was a good idea. Hadn't she just come to the conclusion it was time to put the past behind her? He'd made no promises, and he was going back to Hawaii in a couple days. She knew she needed to be strong, stand up for herself—not cave. But the chance to enjoy his company—to be held in his arms— one last time, was overwhelming. She looked into those sexy sable eyes, his half smile, and was too helpless to resist his magnetism.

"Make that five-thirty, and I'll meet you there."

He put his arms around her and Makenzie and gave them a gentle group hug, tweaked her daughter's nose, and walked to his car. Makenzie hid her face in Juelle's neck.

Her insides warmed to fever pitch, she closed her eyes, and took a deep steadying breath. She was going to miss him when he returned to Hawaii.

She put Makenzie in her car seat, closed the door, glanced over the top of the car, and met Nora Spear's glaring eyes. The girl's sneer was like a knife twisting in her heart. Before she could slip into the driver's seat, Nora turned and walked away, two of her friends who had been with her at the cemetery, at her side. At least they hadn't approached or yelled out, causing a scene. What would she have done had Nora been brazen enough to confront her? She was glad she wasn't going to find out.

****

Hunter waited on the front porch when Juelle

pulled into the paved driveway of her soon to be new house. Butterflies fluttered inside her stomach. What a welcome. A gorgeous man waiting on her door-step.

"Need help with Makenzie?" Hunter tapped on the back window and smiled at the baby in the back seat. Makenzie clapped her hands and smiled back. Even her daughter was delighted to see him.

Not good.

He opened the door and lifted her out of the car seat. Juelle put Makenzie's diaper bag and the blanket in the seat and lifted it out of the car, and then followed Hunter onto the front porch.

"We can go through the house again before we eat. Leave everything here, I'll get it later. Where do you want to start?"

Juelle pulled the key from her slacks pocket and unlocked the door.

"I feel as if I should be carrying you over the threshold or something." He chuckled and wiggled his eyebrows.

Juelle's heartbeat stuttered. "Wrong occasion."

"Nevertheless, it's a special occasion."

"You have Makenzie. That will do." She held the door open for them, then followed them into the foyer. And stopped and stared. Even though she'd been there before, it was an overwhelming sense of having come home, just knowing it was almost a reality. Almost hers.

"I feel like a kid and want to run through the entire house all at once."

"I'm sure you'll have it looking like a real home soon enough. Do you need help with the move?"

"Not much to take with me, thanks. Katelyn and I

plan to go furniture shopping after the closing."

She took Makenzie from him and led the way down the wide hall toward the bedrooms, Makenzie wiggling in her arms. "There's just Makenzie's things—crib, dresser, those sort of things. I'm sure Sven will help out."

They entered one of the bedrooms with lavender walls and white trim. "This will make a perfect nursery for Makenzie. I love the color, and there's plenty of room for growth. As she gets older I can put a regular bed here and a full size dresser over there." She put her daughter down on the hardwood floor and walked to the walk-in closet.

"She's going to love this when she becomes a teenager." Hunter smiled. "What girl wouldn't?"

"You're very forward thinking for a single guy."

"I have cousins and aunts."

"What, no girlfriend back home?" Good Lord, had she really spoken her thoughts out loud? It was a good thing he was behind her and couldn't see the embarrassment she was consumed with at her stupidity.

"No, Juelle. No one at present." His voice sounded hesitant. "Most of the women I've dated were more interested in having a good time on the beaches and not interested in settling down and raising a family. Unless you count the ones who thought owning a travel agency entitled them to free travel with the owner every other week."

She picked up Makenzie, walked down the hall to the very end, and entered the master bedroom.

"Wow. Spacious. I guess I missed this room during the open house. I hope you're planning on buying a king size bed to put under those skylights?"

She was in trouble. Visions of her and Hunter entwined in each other's arms—and legs—in a king sized bed with a starry night sky peeking through the skylight overhead had her entire body on fire. Speechless, she was more than ready to turn around and head back down the hall.

Hunter walked across to a half wall laid up with white Italian tiles that divided the room. "What's this over here?"

Juelle was stuck in place on the mauve wall-to-wall carpet, images of Hunter and her lying in that imaginary bed still playing out in her mind.

"Look at this. Did you see this on the tour?"

Oh, yes. She'd seen it all right. A walk-in shower, the entire interior covered in white Italian marble, naked goddesses taking center stage in smaller tiles three-quarters of the way up and circling three of the walls. It had been one of the selling points for sure.

"Um, yes. Charming, isn't it?"

He stepped inside the shower stall. She didn't have to imagine what he would look like naked—she'd already seen the real deal. She gulped and then turned her back on him and the vision her mind was conjuring up and headed for the hallway. She had to get him out of the bedroom. The house. The State of Maine before she made a fool of herself again. Inviting him to the house had been a colossal mistake.

She switched Makenzie on to her other hip and walked down the hall toward the kitchen. A kitchen should be a neutral, safe place…, well…, maybe not.

Makenzie clutched Tilley in her arms and clung to her neck, bringing Juelle back to Earth and sane thoughts.

"I should make a list of items I'll need."

He followed her into the kitchen, his hand now on her shoulder. "Do you have something to write on? I have a pen."

His touch had her throat going dry. She stepped aside hoping the zing coursing through her entire body hadn't been noticeable.

"No. I, uh…I'll do it another time. Let's go out back. It's getting late and I need to feed Makenzie."

Juelle gave the kitchen a cursory look, declared it fabulous, and then headed toward the side door.

"I'll get the picnic things and Makenzie's car seat. I'll meet you in the backyard."

Juelle stepped out onto a sprawling stone patio with a full awning over top. The area was landscaped with bedding plants in various stages of bloom. She took a deep breath to clear Hunter McClintock from her space and mind and continued to check out the yard. The warm evening air was soothing. She took in the fenced in lawn and the spacious yard was big enough for a swing set for Makenzie. She would have to buy a few lawn chairs and a picnic table. Someone had mowed the lawn for the open house. Juelle kicked off her shoes and stepped onto the grass. She didn't dare walk on the McClintock Estate's perfectly manicured lawn. Here, she would be able to do what she wanted without a disapproving eye following her every move.

"Here we go. Where do you want the blanket?"

"Anywhere is fine."

He proceeded to set the car seat turned carrier on the lawn, flicked the blanket open, and sprawled it out in the middle of the yard. "How's that? Your magic carpet awaits."

If only.

Juelle settled Makenzie in her seat and then sat on the blanket. She dug in the diaper bag for her daughter's dinner, while Hunter opened the paper sack Mrs. Sullivan had prepared for them. He unwrapped the lobster rolls and put them on paper plates, and then opened the Styrofoam containers of coleslaw, and handed her one.

Hunter took a hefty bite out of the lobster rolls. Juelle's mouth watered, watching him, and it wasn't for wanting one of Mrs. Sullivan's specialties. She held her breath, gulped, as Hunter's lips circled the roll. Her insides squirmed.

She looked away, took a nibble from her own roll, then scooped another spoonful of warmed, mixed vegetable baby food she'd kept in the warming container, and spooned it into Makenzie's waiting mouth. Concentrating on her daughter grounded her emotions.

"Wasn't sure what kind of wine you preferred, so I kept it simple. White zinfandel. I hope that's okay?"

"I'm not an expert. White zinfandel is perfect."

He pulled out two plastic wine glasses, filled them, and handed her one.

"To your new home." He offered a toast. She played along as they pretended to clink their plastic stemware together.

"When do you think you'll be able to move into the house?"

"Not soon enough. Mr. Jordan is expediting the paperwork and closing for me."

A slight humid breeze rustled the leaves on the three maple trees on the far side of the lawn, casting shadows along the edge. Juelle pulled a small lightweight blanket from the bag and tucked it around Makenzie, exchanging the food for a bottle of warm milk. Her daughter's eyes drooped. She adjusted the seat so Makenzie could lay back and sleep in comfort.

They continued eating in silence. The bottle Makenzie was holding slipped from her tiny hands and rolled to the blanket. They laughed together. Juelle picked up the empty bottle and put it, and the remainder of her daughter's meal, back in the bag.

"In regard to my mother's proposal," Hunter said. "I called her after the meeting with Mr. Jordan, to let her know Hunt had left her a large amount of money. Of course, she refuses to accept it."

"Why? It's the least she deserved after he abandoned you and your mother. Was she upset?"

"She doesn't need or want the money. She feels like I do, just the fact that he recognized her by mentioning her in his will was more than she expected after all this time. My mother is a saint. Even before I left the Islands to come here, she encouraged me to face my own demons. Said it would be therapeutic."

"And…?"

He gave her a lopsided grin. Her insides squirmed.

"It's been more therapeutic than you know." He wiggled his eyebrows. She concentrated on finishing the rest of her sandwich. "My mother told me to ask if you would disburse the money where it would most benefit the people of Lobster Cove."

"Me? That's very generous of her. But why me?"

"My mother is wise. She figured Eugenia wouldn't want anything to do with money she'd inherited from Hunt. And, she feels the money belongs to the people of

Lobster Cove, as they were the ones instrumental in helping to make McClintock and McClintock a success—their hard work should be repaid."

"How gracious of her. I can ask Eugenia where she feels it would do the most good."

"You don't think she'll refuse to help us with this task? Knowing it's coming from my mother—Hunt's first wife?"

"Eugenia might be a difficult person most of the time, but if she can help those in need, she'll do it in a heartbeat."

"What about you? Do you have any ideas?"

"There are a few places that always need assistance—organizations like the local food pantry, the library, the school. I know Eugenia has helped others on occasion, including the Fisherman's Bereavement Fund and the McClintock Scholarship Fund she created."

"They all sound worthy. I'll check with my mother and see what she thinks."

"And I'll double check with Eugenia. It might be the olive branch needed to smooth things over between you."

"I doubt that is ever going to happen. Especially once the DNA tests are confirmed."

"I don't know, I think her heart scare might have given her something to think about. She was genial when I visited her last night. Günter Jordan stopped by with a bouquet of roses. I think she actually blushed."

"That reminds me…" He reached into a bag and presented her with a small potted plant. "Your new house needs a plant. Consider it a house warming present."

Speechless, she could only stare. Other than her grandparents, no one had ever surprised her with gifts, no matter how small. Her heart melted. It may be insignificant to some, but to her, it was a big deal. Where was this guy two years ago? Why hadn't she met him instead of Sebastian? Her heart ached knowing he was leaving town—leaving her behind. Oh, my God. She had fallen in love with him, and he was leaving. Tears pooled in her eyes.

She reached for the plant only to have Hunter set it aside and draw her across the blanket into his arms. His warm lips on hers sent sparks hitting every nerve in her body.

"You're welcome," he breathed against her mouth and pulled her closer. She clung to him and kissed him back, more urgently this time, a spine tingling longer embrace. They fell toward the ground, his hand protecting her neck, and the other splayed across her back, guiding her to a more comfortable position. Her body was on fire for this man whose touch she couldn't resist.

The sun had disappeared over the top of the trees, the air warm and sensual as it whispered around her sensitized body. She quickly glanced at Makenzie snuggled in her seat—she was content and secure. She glanced up at Hunter and found his eyes full of desire, silently questioning her. Despite her resolve, she was finding it hard to resist him. She craved one more taste of paradise to hold onto for when he was gone—something to keep tucked in her heart. She lifted her lips to his, her hands pulling his head down to meet them in an embrace that was filled with the passion she could no longer hide. Thankfully, Hunter didn't hesitate, his hands finding every erotic spot she never knew she had. The man made her feel things no one ever had.

****

Hunter had been patient long enough. Juelle McClintock was a sea siren—had driven him crazy, calling to him since the first day he laid eyes on her. After making love with her the other night, she was all he'd been able to think about. She was in his arms, now, and she wasn't pushing back. In fact, her kisses were loaded with enough sexual sparks to burn her new home down. And what they did to him was illegal.

He had told himself he wasn't going to make love to her again—there was no way he wanted to hurt her. She knew he was leaving, but he hadn't been able to keep from kissing her, touching her one last time, and damned if he wasn't about to lose control just holding her in his arms—he wasn't going to let go. He couldn't get enough of her, but would she resist if he continued to play out the fantasy he'd been having about her…them…in that shower big enough for two—their bodies naked, sudsy, and slick with lust—and that bed…under the skylight…

She pulled his lips to hers—it took his breath away. He pressed his body against her soft curves, tugged on her hips—she arched into him. Yes! She was on the same wavelength.

"Hmmm, Hunter…"

"Hmmm?" He didn't want to remove his lips from hers, break the connection they were having at the moment. He shifted slightly in case he was too heavy against her. Then rolled her to the side with him. He groaned when her legs curled around his. The lady was

going to kill him before they managed to make love—
he couldn't wait. He ran his hands over her breasts,
down her waist, her hips, her thighs, and groaned. He
nuzzled her neck—her moan as she tightened her arms
around his neck had him growing hard.

He didn't know where this was headed, but he
damn well wasn't going to stop now. Not unless she
stopped him within the next two seconds.

Like the other night, she reached for his belt. He
stopped her long enough to sit back on his haunches
and proceeded to unbutton her blouse. It slid down over
her shoulders. He didn't hesitate, he slid her bra straps
down over her silky smooth shoulders and caressed
them with his lips. He felt her breasts against his chest
and within seconds, they were both naked, back on the
blanket, and in each other's arms.

"Hunter?"

"Hmmmm?"

"Don't stop now. Please."

"I'm no genie, but your wish is about to be
granted."

Chapter Twelve

Juelle carried Makenzie upstairs and laid her in the crib. She tucked her in, gave her a soft kiss on top of her head, and then shut the light switch off on her way out. How could she feel like her world was finally falling into place, her heart soaring on cloud nine, when she knew having made love to Hunter McClintock, again, was wrong on so many levels?

She wanted to chalk it up to being a grieving window—lonely, distraught, needing a comforting shoulder to cry on. But she couldn't. The only grieving she felt was for the loss of life—Sebastian's—not the widow part. Their love had faded long ago. He'd been having an affair. She had only met Hunter a few days ago—it was too soon to fall under his spell and into his arms, let alone have sex with the man—twice. He was flying back home soon—she wasn't into one night stands.

She headed for the shower, but got side-tracked and sat on the edge of the bed. Oh, my, God! Her daughter had been sleeping several feet away while they had made love. What kind of a mother was she? Granted her daughter had been sleeping and unaware. It was all Hunter's fault. He'd hypnotized her into a state of forgetfulness—her surroundings, her daughter, her problems. And yes, she'd lost her mind. But, dear Lord, her mind had returned, and there was no way she could forget what the two of them had shared. Yes, there had been an instant attraction between them—an attraction she had tried hard to ignore. But he'd kept coming to her aid—she should have been on alert to…, what? That he was drawn to her? Felt sorry for her? Wanted her? Like she wanted him? Loved him.

She jumped from the bed and stepped into the shower, her guilt following right behind. She turned on the water and stood under the stinging spray. She shampooed her hair, rinsed, and then let the warm water run over her body, suds pooled around her feet. Was it a mistake? She didn't want it to be. Guilty? For sure. Regrets? She pondered on that one for a moment, smiled, and then with a definite nod, decided she had no regrets. None. Hunter was a very gentle sexual lover, and there had been nothing tawdry about his love-making. He'd made her feel cherished…loved…alive.

She stepped from the shower, grabbed a towel, dried off, and put a nightdress on over her damp head. After blow-drying her hair, she padded across the floor to the bed and stopped. No way could she lie in this bed—a bed she'd shared with Sebastian—after having made delicious, all-consuming love with Hunter moments ago.

She threw on a robe, trooped to the front room where she sat, and looked out over the harbor. Sleep was the furthest thing from her mind. Instead, she could only think about being held in Hunter's arms. How he made her feel, the fire he ignited inside her—a slow burn at first, a rekindling of a glowing ember lit so bright they'd had a hard time putting it out. She sighed, sat back in the chair, and wondered if she'd done the right thing. Was it too soon to be falling in love with

Hunter McClintock? No…yes…*NO!* Just the thought of being held in his warm, strong, sensual arms, his tenderness as he made love to her, caused tears to form in the corner of her eyes. The lights on the harbor glistened as she focused on them. Tried to control her chaotic emotions.

She would never be able to go in the backyard of her new house again without the memory of the two of them making love under the moonlight in the middle of the lawn. She looked down at the rings Sebastian had placed on her finger two years ago.

It was time.

Juelle didn't hesitate—she slipped the rings off, held them between her fingers, and gazed at them, contemplating what they had meant to her versus what they had meant to Sebastian. To her, they had been everything. But they were a lie. She fisted the rings, held them, holding in the anger that had been welling deep inside since the funeral and Nora Spears' outburst. She had to let go of her anger or it would destroy her. She had a daughter to take care of, to love and protect.

Unable to stop them, tears streamed down her face. It was time to let go.

****

Hunter whistled as he walked down to the end of the Frenchman Bay Motel veranda to his room. Instead of going inside, he sat in the outdoor chair, propped his feet up on the foot rest, and smiled. The harbor lights sparkled, his insides hummed. His smile broadened. Juelle was everything he'd envisioned as a sexual partner, their time had been an eye-opening experience—this time was special. She hadn't disappointed. She was warm, willing, and with him every step of the way. But their lovemaking had been much more than sex—she was a very sensual woman, once she allowed herself to give in to her feelings and set her guilt and inhibitions aside. Good, God. What the woman did to him—her touch was like a torch burning him up. Her kisses…whoever penned the phrase sweeter than honey sure did know what they were talking about. God, he was like a corny teenager all over again. He was in love.

Love? Not possible. He was leaving. He couldn't be in love with Juelle. Could he?

He smiled, closed his eyes, and pictured the two of them on that blanket. They hadn't been on it long—rolling into the sweet smelling grass was like an aphrodisiac. Or was it her womanly scent making his heartbeat go wild? He'd take making love on the blanket next to a motel room, any day.

He hadn't wanted to let her go—could have stayed right there in her arms all night long. But the air had cooled their naked, sated bodies, putting a damper on their emotions. And damn, they had forgotten Makenzie was nearby until she whimpered. Juelle's breathtaking body had tensed, and he wanted to kick himself, knowing she was going to be full of guilt.

While she methodically took care of Makenzie, he'd collected the remains of their impromptu picnic, and followed her to their cars. He'd waited until she had the sleeping baby buckled into the back seat, and then he gathered Juelle into his arms again. And couldn't help himself—he kissed her. He smiled again just thinking it had literally knocked his socks off—yes! The woman wanted him again.

****

169

Juelle entered the Lobster Cove Grocery Mart, secured Makenzie in the cart, handed her Tilley the Teddy Bear, and wheeled the grocery cart inside. The baby supply section was two aisles over. She needed jars of junior foods even though Makenzie was well on her way to eating adult foods. Once her teeth came in, she would be able to eat a wider selection of table food. After adding several packages of disposable diapers, wipes, baby oil, and powder, she rolled the cart around the corner, deciding to stock up on cleaning supplies for the new house. As she rounded the aisle, she bumped into another cart.

"I'm so sorry." Juelle looked up from watching Makenzie, smack-dab into Nora Spears' frosty blue eyes.

"You!" Nora turned her cart and headed in the opposite direction, just missing a stock boy shelving paper towels.

"Nora! Wait!" Not thinking if she was making a mistake by following Sebastian's mistress, Juelle followed the tall blonde with her cart. She had to clear the air—after all, they were bound to meet up again— Lobster Cove was a small community and the two of them couldn't duck and dive around each other the rest of their lives—not to mention in grocery stores. "Nora. Please, wait."

"Stop following me," the woman snapped, and then stopped at the end of the aisle, positioning her cart in front of her so Juelle couldn't get by, and glared. "What is it you want? Haven't you done enough?"

Juelle wasn't sure what Nora meant to imply, but it sounded as if she had been the one to cheat on Sebastian. She didn't take the time to count to ten, but she wanted to. Instead, she held her breath for a fraction of a second before she lost control.

"I don't want to cause a scene. What is done is done. I just wanted to make sure you understood that I didn't request the hospital take Sebastian off life support. There is no way I could have done that and let my daughter grow up knowing I was responsible for making that choice."

She waited for a reaction. Nora stood motionless, defiant. Juelle sighed, and then continued.

"Had Sebastian lived, I was going to divorce him. Had he truly loved me, he never would have cheated on me with you."

"He loved me—he was going to divorce you…"

"I wish he had. Maybe it would have saved us all a lot of heartache."

Tears rolled down Nora's pale face leaving trails down through her perfect makeup. Juelle wanted to cry right along with her, but she had no tears left.

"I know we can't be friends, but I hope we can both get past this—I'm sure we'll be running into each other on occasion. Again, I'm sorry for your loss."

Nora nodded, wiped her face with the back of her shaking hand, and walked out of the store, her cart left behind.

Juelle drew in a deep, steadying breath. So much for trying to make peace—at least Nora wasn't ranting and raving like a lunatic this time.

On unsteady legs, Juelle gripped the cart handle and maneuvered her cart around Nora's abandoned one, and wheeled Makenzie toward the checkout counter.

"I'm so proud of you, my dear," Helen Troy, the store's owner said, blocking her way next to one of the pastry tables in the center of the exit lane. "You handled the situation very well. That Nora Spears and her friends are so full of themselves. They are a rowdy bunch. It is such a nice change to see a young person like yourself not feel as if they need to have a shouting match in the middle of my store. My condolences on your loss, by the way. Such a young man to come to a terrible end. How sad. It was a lovely service and so nice of the Ladies of the Rosary Society to purchase all their meat and vegetable platters from my store for the luncheon. And that Father Zack—he did an excellent job, don't you think?"

Mrs. Troy's monologue, although considerate, was worrisome. Would the town gossip spread the word like wildfire? She said the only words that seemed appropriate without adding fuel to Mrs. Troy's fire.

"Thank you, Mrs. Troy. Father Zack did give an excellent service. The Ladies always appreciate the excellent job you do, too."

The woman's smile, as she preened like a peacock, was instant.

"Why, thank you, my dear. I hope your mother-in-law is doing well?"

"Yes, thank you."

With perfect timing, Makenzie broke into their conversation, kicking her feet and swinging Tilley around in the air.

"Oh, my. I've held you up too long. You best take care of this adorable child."

"It is time for lunch."

Mrs. Troy didn't linger, for which Juelle was thankful. She was able to go through the checkout lane without any further confrontations.

When she arrived back at the estate, Juelle put Makenzie down for her afternoon nap, then went in search of Eugenia. It was time to clear the air, let her know she'd be moving out soon. She found her in the arboretum, a tray with her favorite flowered porcelain tea set laid out on the cherry side table.

"Eugenia. May I join you?"

"Yes. I've been meaning to talk to you. I want to spend more time with my granddaughter."

Juelle attempted to keep her face from showing her surprise at her mother-in-law's request and figured she failed.

"That would be wonderful," she said, trying to regain her tact. "Let me know what you have in mind. I just registered her with the Hearts and Hands Child Care Center. I'll be taking her to the center in the mornings. I know you're busy in the afternoons, and some evenings, so if you have something in mind, I can work around your schedule."

"Thank you. She's all I have left of Sebastian."

Juelle wasn't surprised at the connection Eugenia was hanging on to—using Makenzie. She would have to be vigilante and make sure her mother-in-law didn't take advantage of her granddaughter.

"And I would never take her away from you. Günter has assured me I'll be able to move into the house on Aspen Avenue the end of next week. It's not far from here, and you can visit her any time."

"What about McClintock and McClintock? Are you going to keep your half of the company?"

"Yes. That's what I wanted to talk to you about. But first, I wanted to let you know in case you haven't already heard, the Chamber of Commerce voted you in as a life-time member. You should have stayed for the rest of the meeting. The vote was unanimous, and everyone championed your praises."

Eugenia cracked a smile. "I'm getting on in years. Someone else can take over my chairmanship of the Lobster Crawl Committee—someone with more energy. Time for the next generation to get involved. In fact, I'll be stepping back from some of my other committees—I'm not getting any younger."

"Eugenia, you're not old. You are an important part of this community, and people know it. What are you going to do to keep busy?"

"Günter reminded me that I haven't seen much of the world. I aim to see some of it before I grow too old and feeble to enjoy it."

How advanced was Günter and Eugenia's relationship? How long had they had feelings for each other?

"Good for you," was all Juelle could manage.

"I want to know what your plans are for the family business. McClintock and McClintock is an important business here in Lobster Cove."

"Yes, I know. Hunter and I have discussed the situation."

"What are you going to do about the McClintock Scholarship Award Fund and the Fisherman's Bereavement Fund?"

Had Eugenia resolved herself to the notion the business was no longer under her control? Her demeanor indicated as much.

"I'm glad you mention the funds. Hunter and I concurred—you will still control those funds if you wish. They've been a vital part of this community, helping students get an education they otherwise wouldn't have been able to afford—like Keen Quinn and Maya Cruz. And the Fisherman's Bereavement Fund speaks for itself."

"Thank you for that, at least. I would be more than happy to continue on the Board of Directors for those funds, for now."

"There is one issue I would like your input on. Hunter's mother wants to give her inheritance back to the community of Lobster Cove, where it belongs. She asked Hunter to appoint me to disburse her inheritance by donating the money to organizations where it will do the most good. I've already targeted both of your funds anticipating your approval."

Juelle expected Eugenia to bristle at Hunter's mother's request. But she was astonished to see her mother-in-law brighten at the offer.

"That's very thoughtful and considerate of her. And she's right. Her money belongs here in Lobster Cove, not some state that has nothing to do with the McClintock Company."

Eugenia's barb, meant to be considerate, had Juelle mentally shaking her head. Eugenia was Eugenia and would never completely change. But at least she showed her genial side for a change.

"If you're okay with those, I'll let Hunter know. He'll have Günter take care of it. We were wondering if there were other organizations in need you might suggest—ones that would have a greater impact on the community as a whole."

"The food pantry and the Hearts and Hands Day Care run by the Church of God are always in need. Of course the library. Let me think on it, check around, but keep in mind you shouldn't spread the money too thin, so as not to make an impact."

The two sat in silence for several minutes. Juelle was content her mother-in-law was being accommodating in regard to Hunter and his mother's proposal.

"You aren't wearing your wedding rings," Eugenia huffed. "I trust it has nothing to do with Hunter McClintock?"

It didn't take Eugenia long to get around to noticing, or mentioning it and acting her usual grumpy self. Instead of waiting for Eugenia to pounce further, Juelle turned and faced her mother-in-law and held up her hand.

"You have no say in whether or not I have anything to do with Hunter McClintock. Having taken my rings off had more to do with Nora Spears and Sebastian and their affair, than it does with anything or anyone else, including Sebastian's death. Are you sure you didn't know about their affair?"

"No. I was just as astounded as you. I'm sorry, Juelle. We might not have always seen eye to eye, but I wouldn't have wished that on anyone—including Hunt's first marriage. For many years I was unaware he had been married before—or had a son. Hunt was not an innocent in this. He could have spoken up before we were married. I don't know why he didn't. Maybe he thought it was too late. For whatever reason, he did stick by my side. And for that, I've always been grateful."

Juelle wished Hunt had been there for his real son. Eugenia was right—Hunt was not an innocent bystander involving the lives of those around him.

"There is no erasing the past," Juelle offered, wondering how they were all going to carry forward. "We can only look ahead and try not to make the same mistakes. It's time to look ahead—for both of us."

Chapter Thirteen

Juelle felt as if she was on pins and needles. She hadn't seen Hunter since they'd made love in her new backyard, and seeing him now highlighted her desire to be held in his arms again. To taste his kisses. To make love with him one more time, before he left to go back home.

Her insides tensed, she clasped her hands in her lap under the table and prayed Mr. Jordan would put in an appearance soon. Eugenia entered, skirted around Hunter, who sat at the end of the conference table, and walked around to the other side. Hunter nodded in recognition of Eugenia's presence. Eugenia's lips formed a straight tight line as she returned the nod. Just when the air was becoming thick with mild dislike between the two, Mr. Jordan entered the room and sat down at the other end of the table. It felt like déjà vu, it resembled their first meeting in this very room.

"Good afternoon," Günter said. "I have the results of the DNA test the present Mr. McClintock," he paused and swung his right hand in Hunter's direction, then continued, "requested be administered to prove Hunt McClintock is his father, and thus the legal heir, as stated in Hunt's will, and the letter claiming to be his father."

Eugenia twitched in her chair. After the congenial conversation they'd shared, Juelle hoped they weren't going to have a repeat performance of the last time they were all gathered in Mr. Jordan's office. She didn't think Eugenia's heart could take it. When no one spoke, Mr. Jordan cleared his throat, opened the folder he'd carried in with him, and continued.

"Now then, the reports show that in fact, Hunter McClintock is Hunt's son."

Eugenia gasped. Hunter didn't so much as smile or act smug, even though he had the right. Juelle kept her eyes on her mother-in-law. Mr. Jordan wasn't finished.

"As for the paternal confirmation of Sebastian's test, I'm sorry, my dear, but it does verify Hunt was not Sebastian's father."

Tears welled in Eugenia's eyes. She dabbed at them with a hanky. Once again, Günter was at her mother-in-law's side.

"There, there, my dear." He patted her shoulder and knelt down beside her. "This doesn't change a thing. You're well provided for, and Hunt was man enough to keep your secret all these years. He even provided for Sebastian, had he lived. He was a real father to your son all these years."

Eugenia stood and looked at Hunter.

"I'm sorry," she stuttered. "I didn't know he had a child. Edward Miller, Sebastian's biological father worked for Hunt. I found out I was with child after Edward was killed in a car accident. Hunt was kind to me and he seemed so alone. We consoled each other…"

"It's in the past, my dear, it's all over." Gunter continued to pat her hand. "No one else besides the four of us needs to know about this."

Mr. Jordan looked at Hunter for verification, then to Juelle. His eyes pleaded with them to conform to his wishes.

"If I am to take over the company—along with Juelle," Hunter's words were firm, and directed at Eugenia. "It will be with the understanding that everyone knows I'm Hunt's son. As for Sebastian…" he paused, looked at her, then Eugenia, and continued. "There is no need to force the point. I do not intend to make an issue of it, nor will I back down from the truth, should it arise, once I leave this room."

Eugenia inclined her head, wrung her hands, and sat back down. Juelle let out a breath.

Hunter stood and faced the couple across the table.

"Unless you need me to remain to discuss additional business, I'll be leaving."

"Not unless you need assistance in transferring the business."

"Not at this time. I believe you can deal with all the details according to my father's wishes, as well as my mother's request. Juelle and I still need to discuss joint ownership."

"Certainly. I'll contact you when things have been finalized and put in place." Günter stood and walked around the table to Hunter's side. The two men shook hands.

Juelle stood, positioned the chair under the table, and made her way out of the conference room. What did Hunter have in mind? Hadn't they already decided on the joint ownership of the business? The donors for his mother's portion of the inheritance? What was left for them to discuss?

Hunter caught up with her, and ushered her outside. A short afternoon shower had left a rainbow over the harbor, and the fresh scent of washed earth steamed up from the ground as the sun drew the moisture out into the air.

"I'm scheduled to fly home early tomorrow morning. Have dinner with me tonight?"

She found herself nodding, even though it would probably be easier on her heart to say goodbye now. It was official—her world was falling apart all over again.

****

"Juelle, where have you been? You haven't been in for several days. I am so sorry for your loss." Mrs. Sullivan greeted her as she and Hunter entered Mariner's Fish Fry. "Where is that darling girl of yours?"

"Eugenia is babysitting tonight."

"What a lucky grandmother. My daughter should be married and having a baby of her own by now so I could babysit."

"Mother. Please. You know Sven and I are waiting until after I finish my classes." Katelyn approached, carrying a serving tray in her left hand, laden with a bowl of steaming clams. "You sitting outside?" she asked Juelle, as she kept on going to deliver the tray at a table across the room.

"Yes."

"I'll meet you out there," Katelyn called as she shuffled in and out between the tables full of customers.

"Go. Have a seat," Mrs. Sullivan told them. "There are a couple of empty tables left out back. Katelyn will be there. Enjoy."

Hunter followed her through the sliding doors to the deck overlooking the harbor. Her heart beat triple time—Hunter was leaving tomorrow. There had been no talk of his returning. She hadn't made a decision in regard to the company. Would he change his mind? Stay in Lobster Cove and run the business or sell out and she'd never see him again? Her appetite disappeared before they made it to the table in the far corner—the one Hunter had sat at the first night she'd seen him.

They had no sooner sat down then Katelyn slid in next to Juelle. Katelyn wiggled her fingers in front of Juelle—a diamond ring sparkled under the lights strung around the deck.

"It's about time." Juelle hugged her friend. "Have you set a date yet?"

"No, but I wanted you to be the first to know. Well, after my parents of course."

"Congratulations," Hunter offered from across the table.

"Thanks. Can't stay. It's extra busy tonight. The folks are offering their special tonight. So, give me your order and I'll get out of your way." Katelyn wiggled her eyebrows, stood, and pulled out her order pad.

Juelle hid her own ringless hand under the table, and ordered the special, Hunter ordered the same, then sat quietly drumming his fingers on top of the table. What could she say? Stay? Don't go? Take me with you?

He reached across the table and clasped her right hand—she kept her left under the table. She wasn't ready for him to discover she no longer wore her rings. He twined his fingers through hers.

"I hate for us to end this way. I'm sorry, Juelle. But I have to go back home. I have a business to run, my mother is counting on me."

"I understand. You don't owe me any explanations.

You've been kind to me and Makenzie. I don't know how I would have made it through the past couple of weeks without you."

"There was more to our lovemaking, and you know it. I'm sorry I have to leave…"

Their meal arrived, ending whatever else Hunter was about to say. She picked at her crab cakes. What little appetite she had before they ordered had disappeared.

"We need to talk." He leaned across the table, looked into her eyes—her soul. "I need to apologize, but it's too noisy here, not enough privacy."

She shook her head. Privacy? Did she dare be alone with him, again? He was leaving. She'd never see him again. Yet, she craved his touch.

She wasn't going to cry. Not here. Not in front of Hunter. She swallowed, forced her voice to sound normal, not emotional. She wasn't going to be one of those emotional women who fell apart and made a scene. She shouldn't have agreed to meet with him tonight. It was only dragging their goodbyes out.

"I understand." She nodded. "If anyone should apologize, it's me. I don't know what got into me—the last few weeks have been difficult, but that's no excuse for the way I acted."

"If you're done eating, so am I. Let's go somewhere more private."

"That's not a good idea."

"But I'm leaving tomorrow…"

She stiffened her resolve, even though she was more than ready to leave the restaurant. "Right. So we might as well say goodbye now."

Hunter threw more than enough money on the table

to pay for their meal, extended his hand across the table in an invitation for her to go with him. Her resolve dwindled. She placed her hand in his and followed his lead. She waved to Katelyn and Mrs. Sullivan as they took the stairs on the outside of the restaurant from the deck leading to the parking lot. Before she had a chance to open the passenger side door, Hunter had her up against the car, his body so tight against hers, his kiss took her by surprise. Oh, God, Maybe her world wasn't coming to an end after all. She kissed him back.

Just when she'd given in and was about to cross the line, again, he pulled back, rested his forehead on hers, and took an unsteady deep breath. He smoothed his hands down her arms, clasped her hands, and lifted them to his lips. His thumb rubbed over her fingers. He froze. Looked deep into her eyes. She read the question in his sexy eyes. He lifted her left hand to his lips and caressed each fingertip, then placed a warm, erotic kiss on the spot where the rings had been. Embarrassed, Juelle started to apologize, pull her hands out of his, but his lips landed back on hers and she was lost all over again.

"I'm sorry," he whispered next to her trembling lips.

She wasn't sure what he was sorry about—that they had made love? Or that he was leaving?

"I wish things were different." He leaned against the car. "Have you made up your mind what you want to do about the business?"

Really? After his explosive kiss, after the mind-blowing lovemaking they'd shared? That's what he was concerned about? He was leaving her and he wanted to know about lobster fishing?

"I don't want any part of it, but I have to think of Makenzie. I'll hang on to it for now. Like you suggested." Which meant she would have to work with him, see him again at some point? "What about you? Are you going to keep your half?"

"For now. If you change your mind, and hear of anyone wanting to buy us out, let me know. You have my number."

They were both quiet for a moment, as he continued to hold her hand, rubbing his thumb over the inside of her wrist. Her heart was breaking.

"What about the house? Is Jordan taking care of everything for you—everything in order?"

"Yes. Everything will be finalized by the end of next week—it'll be all mine."

"I'm sorry I won't be around to help with the move."

"I understand. You have a business, a life to get back to in Hawaii."

"Juelle…"

"Don't. I understand. It was a mistake to think your concern meant more than it did."

"I never meant to hurt you…, never meant to lose control. Sebastian was a jerk. You need time to come to grips with everything you've been through, get your life back together. Make a life for you and Makenzie."

"I'll be fine. Really. Thanks for being there for me when I needed someone." She tugged her hand out of his, circled to the driver's door, and regarded him over the top of the car. "Goodbye, Hunter. Have a safe flight home."

****

The warm tropical breeze off the Pacific Ocean

greeted Hunter the second he stepped off the plane onto the hot tarmac. He'd always breathed a warm sigh of relief when he returned from the latest tour, but today his heart was heavy. He had mixed feelings about leaving Juelle McClintock behind in Lobster Cove. What was it about her that had gotten so entrenched inside his heart he hadn't been able to guard his emotions?

He'd always been good at not connecting on an emotional level. With Juelle, it was way beyond feeling sorry for her and the loss of her cheating husband. He'd promised himself she wouldn't be hurt by another McClintock, and he'd broken his promise. He'd seen it in her beautiful tear-filled, sea-green eyes he couldn't get out of his mind every time he closed his own eyes. But he had a business to run here in Hawaii—there was no way he would leave his mother in the lurch—she'd been there for him all these years. McClintock and McClintock Lobster Company back in Maine was in excellent hands with Coleman Baker. Juelle's finances were in good shape, thanks to Hunt's will. She had her daughter, a new home, and a new life.

She didn't need him.

Hunter found his mother at their travel office in the Waikiki Shopping Plaza on the corner of Kalakaua and Seaside. They had rented an office in the upscale shopping center five years ago, making it easier for tourists to locate them and book trips. As usual, she sat at her desk mapping out tours.

"It's late. You should be home relaxing."

"Hunter! You're back." She rounded the desk littered with spreadsheets and gave him a warm hug. "Aloha. I have missed you."

"You're looking much better. How are you feeling?" He hugged her in return. Waited until she sat down and relaxed, and then sat in the chair on the opposite side of her desk.

"The doctor said I am fine. It was just a bad case of flu. Now, tell me everything. Did Hunt's wife accept my offer to return the money to Lobster Cove?"

"Juelle, Sebastian's widow, talked to Eugenia. I understand she took it well, and didn't flinch once she learned the money was being given back to the community, as well as the funds she controls. According to her, Eugenia has a soft heart when it comes to the community of Lobster Cove. Of course, she wasn't very welcoming when she spotted me." It was an understatement, but his mother didn't need to know the full particulars. It would serve no purpose.

"I have a letter for you from Hunt." He drew it out of his shirt pocket and handed the folded envelope to his mother. He wasn't surprised when she didn't take it right away. He still hadn't read the letter from his father. He hadn't made up his mind whether or not he wanted to. It was in his travel bags. "If you don't want to read it, you don't have to. But take it and decide later. He also left one for me. I haven't read it yet."

She accepted the envelope with reluctance, laid it on the desk, and stared at it. Her face turned pale. *Damn.* He should have waited until she was at home alone and not likely to be disturbed by clients and could deal with it on her own terms.

"I'm sorry. I didn't want to give it to you at all, but then, it's not my place to make these decisions."

"No need to apologize, son. I am anxious to read it—find out what happened all those years ago. Why he never contacted me."

It didn't matter what his father's excuses were, he'd broken his mother's heart. No matter what his father had to say, it wouldn't erase or alter his callous actions of the past. His abandonment of his wife, Hunter's mother—and him. Not now, after all these years? His respect and love for his mother grew even more—she was a strong, resilient woman. He was proud of her. She reminded him of Juelle—she was also a strong, resilient woman—she would be just fine without him.

"So, tell me, are you now the owner of the lobster business in Maine, or did you turn your half over to Juelle McClintock?"

"Like I told you on the phone, I am now the proud owner…joint owner…of the McClintock and McClintock Lobster Company. We, Juelle and I, have decided to let it run with the current operators and see how things go. Coleman Baker has a good handle on the business. There is no need for either Juelle or me to interfere at the moment. We took a tour of the facilities and everything is intact, running smoothly, and there isn't much we need to do at the moment. I can check in with the manager on occasion from here."

"What about your partner—Juelle McClintock?"

What about her? He hadn't stopped thinking about her since boarding the plane to come home. "She's found a house for her and her daughter, Makenzie. Cute little tyke. Mr. Jordan, their lawyer, is helping to expedite the closing so she can settle in by the end of next week. It's a nice modern ranch style home with a large yard in a good location."

His mother's smile held a trace of smugness he

ignored. "So what's on my agenda? What tours do you have scheduled for me to lead?"

"You changed the subject. This girl is not so easy to forget, I take it?"

"No. She's not easy to forget. But there is nothing between us, so get that look off your face."

"A mother can only hope. Hunter, you have dragged your feet for so long. It is time for you to think beyond work. Find yourself a nice girl and settle down. Don't keep things bottled up inside. What happened between me and your father is not going to happen to you. I was just as much at fault. I didn't pursue Hunt after he left. If you love someone, do whatever it takes. You go after her."

"She has a life in Maine. Not Oahu."

Their eyes met. She raised her eyebrow, and smiled. "Perhaps your feelings aren't as strong as you think they are—as strong as they should be. But if they are, do not make the mistake of walking away. It is your decision, after all."

He wasn't going to comment either way. Instead, he reverted the subject back to the travel schedule.

"What tour do you have me scheduled for? Is it on Oahu, or the Big Island?"

She hesitated, then handed him a sheet of paper with an itinerary on it. "It's the Oahu Island Tour. This one is a two-day tour. We've made hotel reservations on the other side of the island close to the Polynesia Culture Center."

"I'm assuming that's on the agenda?"

"Yes. People don't like to be rushed at the center, so we've scheduled the entire day there, and then an evening luau. There are several stops at some of the

189

more scenic lookouts, and a stop at one of the pineapple plantations. Make sure they have a chance to taste the pineapples while they're there."

"What about Diamond Head Crater and the U.S.S. Arizona?"

"They are your first stops. Tour starts day after tomorrow morning at eight. It's a small group of twenty-four, so I've arranged a small coach. You can pick up the head sets and paperwork the night before."

For the first time since joining the Lani Aloha Travel Agency, Hunter didn't look forward to trooping around the island with a group of twenty-four eager tourists.

Chapter Fourteen

Juelle picked up Katelyn to go shopping for furniture. They followed Route Three across the bridge to the mainland and the Town of Trenton, leaving Mount Desert Island behind. The weather was a typical misty morning with the sun pulling the dew from the earth. A slight breeze brought the damp earthy scents swirling, mingling with a brand new day. Juelle's spirits lifted. She'd been looking forward to shopping for furniture for her new home. Having Katelyn accompany her was sure to make the day a pleasant one—get her mind off Hunter.

"Thanks for the information about the Hearts and Hands Child Care Center. I contacted Jolene Graham and made arrangements to enroll Makenzie on a trial basis. I dropped her off this morning for a trial run—see how she likes it."

"Did she fuss when you left?"

"She started to pucker up, but Carolyn Clark, an elderly lady who works there part time, was like a grandmother, and whisked her away to join the others. She was laughing by the time I shut the door behind me. I think this is going to work out just fine."

"Speaking of grandmothers, how'd it go the other night? Makenzie survive Eugenia?" Katelyn chuckled.

"Yes, they both did fine. Although I had Makenzie in her jammies, fed, and a bottle ready before I left, so

Eugenia didn't have much to worry about. Just rock her to sleep."

"How did Eugenia take the news when you told her you were moving out the end of the next week?"

"She was unusually quiet. At first I wondered if I was doing the right thing by taking Makenzie away from her, even though Eugenia hasn't been your typical grandmotherly type—something that always surprised me. I think her background might have had something to do with her not wanting to get close to others."

"Seems to me she'd be more affectionate, not having had a loving environment growing up."

"She's afraid of the attachment. She's already lost two of the most important people in her life—three if you count Sebastian's father."

"Wait a minute. What about Sebastian's father?"

"Oops. Not for public knowledge. His father's name was Edward Miller. He was killed in a car accident not knowing Eugenia was pregnant. They weren't married. He worked for Hunt on the docks. Do you know the family? Are they from around here?"

"You're making me want to feel sorry for the woman. No, the name isn't familiar. Probably someone who came in looking for a job. There were a lot of young men coming in to work for McClintock's."

They drove in silence for a while, Juelle concentrating on morning traffic.

"Have you heard from Hunter? How are you doing since he left Lobster Cove?"

Katelyn couldn't hold her curiosity in any longer. Juelle hadn't expected it to take her best friend this long. Her friend was nothing, if not direct—the one thing Juelle had learned since meeting her when she'd arrived on the Island with Sebastian. But it was the one thing she loved about Katelyn, as well as trusting her friend to keep her mouth shut when it came to personal secrets.

"Juelle," her friend prompted when she didn't answer right away.

"No. I knew from the beginning 'it' was going nowhere. I was stupid to let myself get involved."

"The heart wants what the heart wants."

"Give me a break. Quotes?"

"Well, it's true. I bet your heart wants Hunter McClintock. I can't think of another reason why you didn't sell him your half of the company."

"It was a 'win-win' to hang on to it for a while. At least until things settle down and I see what Makenzie and my needs are."

"Yeah. Right. You don't want to let go of Hunter McClintock."

Was Katelyn right? Was she holding on, hoping a miracle would transport him back to Lobster Cove? If he didn't sell his half, did she have half a chance? Probably not. Even though they had made love, he hadn't said he loved her. He'd made no promises that he'd return. He'd said he could run his business from afar. All indications were that the minute he'd stepped on the plane to go back to Hawaii, he'd forgotten all about her. He hadn't contacted her, and it had been three days.

Despite her aching heart, the shopping trip turned out to be productive. They found a comfortable living room ensemble, complete with an oak coffee table and matching end tables, two table lamps, a floor lamp, and a bookcase that would fit in the alcove. When they got to the bedroom furniture, Juelle spotted a king size bed. Hunter's comments when they had picnicked at the house had her imagining Hunter and her making love in it, which had her temperature rising.

"Oh. Just the bed for you. Look at it—plenty of room for making all kinds of kinky sex. That's the bed Sven and I need when we get married."

"More info than I needed, Katelyn. Get real. I'm not planning on sharing a bed with anyone in the near future.

"Really? You aren't envisioning you and Hunter doing the 'deed' in that bed? You can't hide that bright shade of pink on your cheeks creeping clear to your neckline."

"Wishing won't make it so. He's gone. History. I have to think about Makenzie."

"If you don't add the bed to the rest of your order…"

"Even if I bought it, doesn't mean I have sexual fantasies about me and Hunter McClintock."

"Liar. Don't think I haven't noticed that you took your rings off. Did you and Hunter have sex already?"

"Katelyn! Hush! Someone will hear you."

Katelyn lowered her voice. "What? You don't have to act so shocked. It was very evident the way the two of you acted at the restaurant the other night. Why, you couldn't stop making eyes at each other like a couple of love-sick teenagers. I'm happy for you. Really. Sebastian was all wrong for you from the beginning."

"I wish I'd known about Nora Spears earlier—it would have saved us both a lot of heartache."

"Have you seen her since the funeral?"

"Only from a distance, after the funeral. And then I

ran into her with my cart at the Grocery Mart the other day. I reiterated I had nothing to do with Sebastian's death, and that I was sorry for her loss."

"Again. You are too kind."

"Like I told Nora, we have to live in the same small community. I don't want to be on guard every time I go out and about and run into her."

"Ladies, have you made a decision on a bedroom suite? Can I show you something else? We have a large selection over here—a gorgeous white French provincial canopy set just around the corner," the saleslady intervened.

"Thanks, but I think Ms. McClintock will take this one." Katelyn's smile could only be described as the cat having stolen the cream and licked the platter clean.

****

The young college girls from Michigan hung on his every word, found ways to walk beside him, touch him, flirt with him, and even get creative in ways to invite him to share their beds. He wasn't interested. He'd always been careful not to cross that line, but they were even more obvious now that he wasn't interested in flirting back.

When they arrived at the Polynesian Cultural Center, he let the group go off on their own, giving them a time to gather back at the Theater for the cultural show and the luau. Established by the Church of Jesus Christ of Latter-day Saints, it was a non-profit, educational and cultural interactive center and was meant to maintain the individual cultures. He'd guided this tour so many times, he could walk through each and every separate village and every inch of the center blindfolded. The Pageant of the Long Canoes was always a big hit. The individual canoes were as colorful, musical, and as individual as the islands they represented—Samoa, New Zealand, Fiji, Tahiti, Marquesas, Tonga, and of course, Hawaii.

He found an empty bench under a shade tree, sat down, and set his travel bag on the ground next to his feet. He leaned back, crossed his leg up over his knee, and perused the tropical paradise that surrounded him. Would Juelle like it here? Would she be interested in living in Oahu? Raise Makenzie in this tropical paradise? He pictured them on the beach, bonfires in the evening under the star-studded sky? Walking hand in hand in the warm foamy Pacific waters?

Could he live in Maine?

He took his cell out and considered calling Juelle back in Lobster Cove. Was his mother right? Should he pursue Juelle? Did he love her enough to want to spend the rest of his life with her? To take a chance at a permanent relationship? Did she love him? Had she moved on? Found someone else? He put the cell back in his pocket and sat for a few more minutes without seeing the tourists walking past, wondering if he should read the letter from his father? It was tucked in his business pouch he carried with him on tour. He pulled it out, rubbed his hand over his face. What to do? Was he about to open a can of worms?

He slit the top of the envelope open and took out the folded letter. It was written with the old-style fountain pen and ink, the scrawling penmanship clearly legible. He wondered when his father had written it.

My son: I can only offer the truth of the matter for not having you and your mother in my life. Your mother was a fine woman, and I

196

was wrong to think she would fit in with my life here in Lobster Cove—the winters can be very harsh for a fragile Hawaiian. My father was a formidable, demanding man, and I was a weak youth who had no control over his life. I was foolish to think your mother would survive the hardships I faced on a daily basis, knowing how my demanding father would crush her dynamic spirit—the spirit I fell in love with. Although we married, I had no knowledge of a child until it was too late.

When I returned to Lobster Cove, my father forced an annulment. I tried to contact Lani, wrote several times, but never heard from her again. I could only assume she wanted nothing to do with me. It wasn't until after I remarried that I learned of your existence. In my heart, I felt confident Lani would raise a fine son, and that you and your mother were much better off in Hawaii without me. I don't ask for forgiveness—I have done nothing to deserve it, but know your mother was in my heart until the very end.

Hunter crumpled the letter in his hands. His father was right in many respects—he had grown up with a wonderful, loving mother and family. He wouldn't have traded it for anything in the world. Was he sorry he hadn't had a chance to know his father?

He looked around the Polynesian Cultural Center, considered the many opportunities that had come his way over the years, the friends, the travel, and his life here on the islands—he was happy. And although his father's letter was enlightening, it didn't excuse his father's lack of manhood—sticking up for what he believed in, wanted with all his heart. Could he have defied a father like Hunt's father? Fight for the woman he loved? Was his mother right—if you want something bad enough you go after it?

"Perhaps your feelings aren't as strong as you think they are—as strong as they should be. But if they are, do not make the mistake of walking away. It is your decision, after all."

Was he as blind and obstinate as his father? Had he left the woman he loved behind because he had no backbone? Afraid to commit?

The colorful Pageant of the Long Canoes wound their way through the waterways and lagoons. Each was filled with dancers and music representative of the islands they represented here at the center. Visitors rushed to the benches and along the shore to watch one of the more popular events at the Center. The clapping, music, singing, picture taking, and gaiety failed to interest him for the first time since he'd been doing this particular tour. He was thankful his tour group was scheduled to meet at the theater for the afternoon show—he wasn't looking forward to dealing with their many questions, their enthusiasm—his mind was back in Lobster Cove.

Crap. It was going to be a long two days on tour.

Chapter Fifteen

Juelle met the delivery truck when it pulled up to her new home. With Makenzie at the Hearts and Hands for the day, she was free to instruct the men on where to place her new furniture. In no time, everything was right where she had envisioned it. She signed the delivery form, thanked the men, and waved as they got in their truck to leave. She closed the door, leaned against it, and smiled. She and Katelyn had hung curtains, and the draperies had been installed yesterday. She was all set to move in with Makenzie tomorrow.

She walked through the house, loving every little nuance—the kitchen, living room, nursery, and even the spacious laundry room. She found herself in the master bedroom staring at the bed Katelyn had talked her into buying. It was too big for just one person, and she didn't think that would change for a long time to come. Tears formed, but before she let them fall, she walked out of the room and back down the hall.

The doorbell rang just as she entered the living room. Thinking the delivery men had left something behind, she hurried to open the door and found Hunter McClintock standing on her porch, hands behind his back, a silly grin on his face.

"Aloha," he said, and offered a multi-colored lei of small orchids from behind his back. He placed it around her neck. "I missed you."

Speechless, she stared at his handsome features. She had missed him, too. Dreamt of him every single night since he'd gone back to Oahu. But what was he doing in Lobster Cove? Was something wrong at the company? Did he want to get rid of his half? Sell the company and needed her permission? The indecisive look on his face made her uncomfortable. Before she could ask any of her questions, he leaned in and gave her a quick, almost nervous kiss, as if he wasn't sure it would be welcomed.

"It's tradition to kiss the recipient of the lei."

"What are you doing here?"

"I have something to ask you…"

"You can have my half of the business, if you want it. I don't need or want it."

He kissed her again, crushing the flowers against her chest. Heaven help her, her arms circled his neck. The fresh scent of crushed orchids enveloped them. She leaned into him, her insides exploded, her mind a blank. She didn't care why he had come back to Lobster Cove, she was too caught up in being held in his embrace. His kiss softened, a warm shockwave vibrated clear down to her toes and back up through her inner core. She gasped when he lifted her off her feet and carried her into the house. And kicked the door shut. The implications not lost on her addled brain, she wiggled in his arms until he let her down.

"Hunter…?" She stepped out of his arms, put enough space between them so she could breathe again. His gaze locked with hers.

"I've missed you, Juelle. You and Makenzie. You're all I've been able to think about since I left Lobster Cove—night and day. I had to come back to you—I couldn't desert you like my father deserted my mother. I love you—and if you love someone, you don't let them go, you follow them. You don't shut them out of your life."

Oh, my, God! Did he just say he loved her?

"I've missed you too…"

"Say it. Say you love me…"

"I love you."

She was back in his arms, his lips on hers. He lifted her once again and twirled her around the room.

"I have it on very good authority that there is a king-sized bed in the other room just waiting for us."

"What? Whose authority?" She snuggled in his arms, her head in the crux of his neck, his firm, strong body sending her signals she had no trouble deciphering.

"I ran into Katelyn and Sven. Are you going to invite me into that bed?"

He was already heading down the hall with her still in his arms before she consented. He kissed her on the forehead, sat her down at the foot of the bed, and joined her, his arm circling her waist.

"I have to ask you something before—"

"I told you I don't want the business."

"You sure? Because it comes with strings attached."

His playful smile turned serious. She stood, wanting to put distance between them again, afraid of what he was about to say. He tugged her hand, bringing her back to his side.

"The only stipulation to go along with the company is that you marry me. I can live without McClintock and McClintock, but I can't live without you."

He lifted her chin, his eyes seeking an answer. She read the truth of his desire and leaned in and pressed his lips to hers.

"Yes. Oh. Yes. I'll marry you."

"I won't let you down—ever again. I swear."

"I have no reason to doubt you.

"How would you like to live in Oahu during Maine's winter months? I have my own house along the coast with a private beach. We can keep this house and live here in the summer?"

Tears formed in her eyes. Taken aback at his thoughtfulness, she didn't know what to say. He wiped her tears with his thumbs, and a delicious heat warmed her insides. Juelle didn't know what she'd ever done to deserve his love.

"Or, I can always move here. It doesn't matter to me, as long as we're together."

"Oh, Hunter. I'd love to live in Hawaii, with you. Are you sure?"

"We have a company to run here. It's the perfect solution. But there's one more thing we have to deal with."

Juelle held her breath. The only thing she wanted to deal with at the moment was to be held in his arms again. He took her hand in his and looked down at it and then up into her eyes.

"I think you're missing something on that hand of yours. Will this do?" He slipped a single solitaire ring on her finger, lifted it to his lips, and kissed it.

"There. It's official. As soon as we can arrange it, we'll make it permanent. In the meantime, I say we put this bed to good use."

A word about the author...

Carol Henry is an author of Destination: Romance—Exotic Romantic Suspense Adventures, as well as contemporary romance and historic women's fiction. She is an international traveler, and travel writer of exotic locations for major cruise lines' deluxe in-cabin books and Porthole Cruise Magazine.

Carol lives with her husband in the beautiful New York State Finger Lakes region where they are surrounded by family and friends.

Find her at: www.carolhenry.org

~*~

Other Carol Henry titles
available from The Wild Rose Press, Inc.
AMAZON CONNECTION
SHANGHAI CONNECTION
RIO CONNECTION
RIBBONS OF STEEL
NOTHING SHORT OF A MIRACLE